MW01138996

STRIKE DRAGON

The Last of the Light

Robert Ashby

Robert Ashby

Copyright © 2022 Robert Ashby
All rights reserved
First Edition

PAGE PUBLISHING
Conneaut Lake, PA

First originally published by Page Publishing 2022

ISBN 978-1-6624-6978-7 (pbk)
ISBN 978-1-6624-6979-4 (digital)

Printed in the United States of America

To my grandma,
Corene Schuble, and my mom
who are always there for me.
Also, to my grandpa Ray Schuble;
my father, Kelly Ashby; and his parents, Bob and Charlie Ashby.
May they rest in peace.
They made me who I am today.

Chapter 1

The fight of the ages between Dragon Knights and the Shadow Dragons, an ancient battle that takes place on the planet called Dragza. Leon Dragon confronted the Shadow Dragon's lair on his own as a "one-man army." They overpowered him and tried to claim the Spirit Core. They discovered Leon did not have the Spirit Core with him, and they saw it drift into space. They tried to go after it, but Leon stopped them with his last breath. To end the war, he sacrificed his life force to use a technique that destroyed the Shadow Dragon's lair by blowing it up with him inside it. The Dragon Knights who witnessed the explosion cheered for the victory but also mourned Leon's death. To honor Leon, they found the remainder of his body and burned it in tribute. They did not go in search of the Spirit Core because they knew it would reemerge when someone worthy was chosen to be the king of the Dragon Knights.

The Spirit Core was drifting in space, searching for the next chosen one of its power. The crystal came to Earth during the feudal era in Japan. It was worshipped because it came from the sky, and it was put into a Temple of the Gods. Anyone who touches the crystal gets mystical powers. The priest in charge of the temple feared it would fall into the wrong hands. To keep it safe, he built a labyrinth around it and put booby traps for security. For hundreds of years, it was safely kept away where trespassers could not find it.

Chapter 2

Time goes fast and shows how the labyrinth becomes dilapidated. Beams start to fall apart, flowers wilt, days and nights go by faster and faster, etc. Time stops at the present on March 8, 2015. The focus is on a group of archaeologists investigating the Legend of the Holy Dragon Stone. The Holy Dragon Stone got its name from the image of a dragon in the stone holding a heart and myths of its mystical powers. The group searched high and low to find the labyrinth. Some of the group began to doubt its existence. The crystal has been dormant for centuries.

They finally found the Temple of the Holy Dragon. Archaeologists saw a statue of a dragon and the crystal hovering from the dragon's palm. There was a light illuminating from the crystal (no one knew where the light was coming from). The main archaeologist, Roger James, walked slowly up the stairs to get the crystal. Right before he was about to grab it, he noticed that the crystal had a weight trigger. He replaced the crystal on the podium with a decoy crystal of the same weight and volume (with much suspense). Luckily, nothing happened, and he was able to do it without triggering the booby traps. All the archaeologists began to cheer, and he walked down the stairs back toward them. The decoy crystal began to heat up like it was going to explode. The temple and the statue began to crack.

He yelled, "Run!" as the fake crystal exploded, and the temple began to collapse in on itself.

On the way to get out of the crumbling temple, a lot of people died in the booby traps. The rest got out of the rubble with the crystal. Only four out of thirty people survived the ruins.

After the smoke cleared, it shows Roger on the ground, shielding the crystal from the falling rubble. He checked the crystal for scratches or dents and found that the crystal is 100 percent unharmed. He checked on the other members of his crew to make sure they're all right. (It shows the three that are shaken up but alive, also pans over the collapsed temple, showing other members of the crew that didn't make it). He took the crystal and secured it in a compartment in one of their vehicles. He took off his hat and placed it over his heart in a tribute to those who didn't make it.

He asked for a moment of silence and said aloud, "For those we have lost to rest in peace."

He put his hat back on and let the crew know they found what they were looking for, and as soon as they recover all the men that they lost that day, they can return home.

Roger cannot stop looking at the crystal in the plane.

Chapter 3

Roger James has been examining the crystal's properties to find out why the crystal is unique and whether the myths are true about its mystical powers. Roger used an ohm tuning fork on the crystal, and by touching it with the fork, it created a vibration. When it vibrates, the crystal glows with white energy. All the other scientists began to congratulate Roger, but the crystal began to glow brighter and brighter, causing everything electrical in the office to short out. The brightness caused a massive shock wave, breaking all the glass around it, with a dragon roar exploding from it. The noise and the light made all the onlookers drop to the ground, shielding their eyes and holding their ears in an attempt to block out the noise. Things began to fall off the walls and made a mess of the room. All the scientists ran out to avoid getting hurt. The blast caused an electrical magnetic pulse.

Roger went to check on his coworkers outside the building. Once outside, he did not see Lilly. He went back inside and found her hiding underneath a desk and asked if she was okay. She acknowledged that she was. They both looked at the crystal, and they saw it was still glowing heavily. Suddenly, the light began to fade. All the scientists came back in. Lilly tried to explain how the light came from the heavens above. The scientists all started talking at once about what the crystal could be.

They decided to put the crystal on show as the newest exhibit at the museum. They knew it could be dangerous, but they made sure they took every precaution to keep it safe. Roger and Lilly wanted everyone to be able to see the amazing crystal that they found. They also wanted to appear with the crystal to explain and teach all the kids about its history. They also wanted to keep an eye on the crystal and make sure everyone would be safe.

*****

In Escondido, California, on April 8, 2015, Kira Scott woke up at 7:31 a.m., even though he could have sworn that he set his alarm for 7:00 a.m.

He yelled, "What a GREAT way to start my birthday!"

He started freaking out and almost fell out of bed. He started getting ready as fast as he could. His sister was in the shower, so he began waiting for her to be done. He brushed his teeth, took a shower, and got dressed as fast as he could. He ate breakfast as he ran out the door while his parents yelled, "HAPPY BIRTHDAY, KIRA!" He grabbed his bike and started riding to school.

On his way there, he saw a kid playing with a ball that accidentally rolled into the street. The kid started to run after the ball heading toward the street and didn't notice a car coming, and the driver didn't notice the kid. Kira sprang into action and tackled the kid, saving him from being run over. The car hit his bike (totaling it) and the kid's ball was run over as well. The driver didn't even stop to see if they were okay. He just sped off. The kid was crying about his ball, and Kira couldn't stand to see him cry. He offered the kid one of his mom's famous chocolate chip cookies from his lunch. Just before the boy could thank Kira, his mother rushed out of their house to check on her son. Kira assured her that her son was okay. The mother thanked Kira for saving her son, and that somewhat embarrassed Kira.

The bell rang for school and Kira almost swore but instead said "SHOOT!" and ran toward the school. He waved goodbye and apologized for having to leave so quickly. He got into class a minute or two late, and the teacher started yelling at him. Kira tried explaining to the teacher what happened, but the teacher didn't believe him. The teacher let out a sigh and told Kira to take a seat and not let it happen again. He saw his friends, Kari and Chuck, in their seats already. He took his seat, and his friends broke out into a funny version of the "Happy Birthday Song." After they were done, the teacher asked if everyone was ready to go on their planned field trip. Everyone answered yes excitedly.

The teacher informed them, "Today's field trip is to the San Diego Archaeological Center, and there will be a test afterward about what you've learned."

Everyone groaned because they were hoping it would be a fun field trip. However, their teacher made it sound like it wasn't going to be because of the test afterward. Kari was excited to go to the museum. Chuck was messing around with Kira. Kira explained to Chuck and her in more detail what happened with the kid. He remembered that he left his bike in the middle of the street. They praised him and said not to worry, and they would help him get his bike after the field trip ends.

Chapter 4

One of the school bullies tripped Kira and made fun of him, calling him "Cry-ra." As Kira was getting up, he gave the bully a huge glare like he wanted to fight him. He and the bully were about to fight, but Kari got in the middle of it. The bully said that Kira started it. Kari snapped that she didn't care who started it, but she was finishing it. Then she calmed down and checked to see if Kira was all right.

He said, "Yeah, I'm fine. Thanks."

They got in line with Chuck and boarded the bus, and they all sat together. Kira looked like he was half asleep and not as energized as Kari thought he would be. She asked if he was okay.

He said, "Yeah, I had another one of my weird mysterious nightmares last night!"

She asked him what the dream was about. As Kira began to explain the dream, he has a flashback of it.

Kira explained that the dream started with him being in a pitch-black room. The room is completely black until he saw a priest in the corner of the room. The priest's face slowly lights up every time he calls out Kira's name.

He kept asking the priest, "What do you want from me?"

The priest kept calling out Kira's name, and each time, his face lit up.

He kept asking the priest, "What do you want from me?"

Finally, the priest answered, "You're the one, Kira," he said in a mysterious voice as he pointed at him.

Then Kira asked the priest, "The one what?"

The priest replied, "The one who will bring peace to the Multiverse. You will have great power!"

Kira asked, "What kind of power?"

"The power of the light," the priest replied.

The priest vanished into the darkness. Kira ran after the priest to ask him for clarification, but the priest was already gone. The darkness pressed in on him until he noticed tendrils of light creeping around him. He turned around and saw a Dragon of Light about to attack him. Then he screamed and woke up. This dream has occurred every night for the last couple of weeks.

After Kira was done explaining the dream, they arrived at the museum. All the students went inside, and they saw a lot of interesting items, including lots of different crystals. One of the exhibits showed how the archaeologists discovered and categorized the crystals. Kari dragged Kira and Chuck by the arms with her around the museum. All of them were joking around with each other.

After they were done with the exhibits, they looked through the pictures they took together on Kari's phone. She was very happy looking through the photos. Kira was indifferent. She looked up to say something to Kira and noticed a huge poster advertising a new exhibit. She asked the guys if they wanted to go check it out. They didn't really want to see any more exhibits, but she gave them "puppy-dog eyes."

Chuck said, "DON'T LOOK INTO HER EYES!"

Kira said, "Why not?" and he turned to look into her eyes. He saw the look and was like, "Oh no."

Chuck said, "That's why!"

Kira couldn't resist her look and said exasperatedly, "Okay fine. Five minutes."

Kari smiled knowingly and said excitedly, "Come on!"

She then pulled them both through the crowd of students. When they got to the front of the crowd, they saw a huge curtain covering the exhibit with the owner of the museum, Rodger, and Lilly there standing in front of the microphone. The owner of the museum introduced Rodger and Lilly as the cofounders of the Crystal.

They began explaining what they found and how they discovered it. They described the myth of the crystal. Rodger told the kids how the Crystal has mystical powers, and whoever touches the crystal will experience something amazing!

Lilly said, "Ladies and gentlemen, we bring you 'the CRYSTAL OF THE HOLY DRAGON.'"

Rodger pulled the curtain and revealed the crystal in a glass case with a replicated model of the Temple of the Holy Dragon. The entire crowd went OOH and AWWW. Rodger noticed that the crystal is beginning to glow brighter and brighter (which is alarming). Rodger whispered to the museum curator that there is something wrong with the crystal. The curator kept his composure and told everyone to enjoy looking at it and then go enjoy their lunches that the bus drivers have left in the cafeteria for them.

The curator of the museum pulled the archaeologist aside and said, "What do you mean there's something wrong with the crystal?"

Rodger explained that it is not supposed to glow like that, and the only other time he saw it glow that intensely was when the temple began to collapse. He told Rodger and Lilly to keep an eye on it but make sure they didn't cause a panic. The curator, Rodger, and Lilly went back to observe the crowd. They took a seat by the crystal to watch it closely.

Kari was enthralled by the crystal and told Kira that they should take a closer look at it, saying that they should get a glimpse of what it looks like from the other restricted side of the exhibit. He wasn't sure, even though he wanted to investigate it. He didn't think it would be a good idea because he didn't know if there was security. Chuck agreed with him and said it would be a good idea to keep their distance because they didn't want to cause any trouble. Kari made a joke about it being radioactive and teased Kira about being scared.

Chuck said, "If it was really radioactive, how could they get it in here without getting infected?"

Kira suggested a hazmat suit and they all laughed. Kari glanced around and made sure no one was paying attention to her and ducked under the stanchions that cordoned off the crystals. Kira rolled his eyes and went after her, shooting a disapproving look at Chuck. Kari and Kira went up the back stairs to approach the crystal from behind. Kira was trying to convince Kari to go back because he didn't want to get caught. She said she just wanted to get one closer look. He followed her up the stairs to see the crystal. He could see the crystal's light reflecting in her eyes. She felt such a strong connection to it and reached out to touch the glass. Kira came up closer to her, and the crystal began to glow brighter.

She asked, "Did you see that?"

Kira responded, "What?"

She asked him to take a few steps back, and the crystal got less bright. She gestured for him to come forward, and when he stepped forward, it got brighter again. They did this several times, and she believed that the crystal was responding to Kira's presence in some way. Kira got even closer to the exhibit. He was confused and wondering why it reacted that way when he got closer. He saw a shimmering static coming from the crystal. Kari, who had her hand on the glass, removed it and stepped back quickly.

Kira slowly raised his hand up and touched the static. Instantly, he had a vision. The vision was of a great war between dragons. He saw a dark evil warrior attempting to conquer Earth and a planet he had never seen before. The vision showed a Holy Dragon. The Holy Dragon warrior reached out and held the worlds in his hands before the evil warrior could reach them. He reached out for Kira, and he remembered his previous dream.

The vision ended when Kira heard a security guard yell, "Hey! What are you doing back there?"

Kira stepped in front of Kari to protect her. He explained to the security guard that Kari was curious, and they were both sorry.

Kira continued, "Kari and I will go back with the rest of the crowd."

The security guard instead began escorting them out to where everyone was having lunch. The archaeologist, Rodger, grabbed the guard's shoulder, emerging from the darkness. He told the guard that escorting them would not be necessary, and it was okay to be curious. In fact, Rodger explained he was curious too. Rodger said he would appreciate it if the security guard would leave the two of them, so they could have a discussion.

The security guard said, "Okay, but this one's going to cost you $20."

Rodger pulled out $30 and offered it to the guard. "There is an extra $10 for your silence."

Rodger patted the guard's shoulder, and the guard walked away.

Rodger and Lilly approached Kari and Kira and stated that they were curious why the crystal reacted the way it did when Kira approached it.

Kari stated, "You saw that too?"

Rodger explained that they were watching and saw it happen. Rodger wanted to know if Kira would be willing to allow them to conduct studies of his effect on the crystal. Kari told Kira and Rodger that it would be cool if they wanted to figure it out as long as she would be involved too. Kira thought about it for a few moments.

Rodger then said, "It's a deal!"

He offered Kira a handshake. Kira hesitantly glanced at Kari before grasping Rodger's hand in agreement. Rodger told Lilly to get Kira and Kari's contact information. Rodger told them he would be in touch, but for now, they needed to get back to their classmates.

Kari and Kira walked back downstairs and rejoined the crowd, looking for Chuck. They found him and explained what happened with the crystal and the archaeologist in hushed voices.

Chuck said, "You two are so lucky you didn't get in trouble."

Chuck reminded them that they needed to get to the bus before it left. The three ran for the bus and made it just in time. Rodger and Lilly watched as the kids left.

Without anyone knowing, the crystal began to pulsate, and a disembodied voice stated softly, "He is the one."

After the field trip ended, Kira returned home. When he came through the door, his sister, Mia, surprised him with a hug. He asked what the hug was for. Mia told him that it's a special birthday hug for his eighteenth birthday. He looked around and noticed that his parents threw him a surprise party, complete with a cake and singing. Kira got a lot of awesome presents, including the brand-new mountain bike he had been asking for. His mom asked where his old bike was because she didn't see it outside and asked him if he wanted to keep the old bike too.

Kira chuckled and scratched the back of his head. "I definitely won't be keeping the old bike…" With his mother's confusion, he said, "Long story, Mom. I'll tell you about it later." And then chuckled again.

During dinner, Kira's father took him aside and asked him to partner with him at a karate tournament that was coming up. He agreed and decided that he would need to get ready for it. He had been waiting for a moment like this to be in a tournament with his father. His father told him to train hard but not overwork himself like he did back in the day. Kira told him not to worry about it.

Kira began training a lot that night for the tournament. The only technique he had trouble with was the split kick. He practiced the split kick over and over that night until his foot was sore. He had to call it quits for the night. He climbed up on his bed and the last thoughts in his mind before he fell asleep was that strange crystal. The crystal was being protected and monitored by several security guards.

One of the guards said, "All clear! Everything is okay."

The other security guard passed by the crystal once more before he went to eat his snacks on a bench on the second floor. The other guard continued to walk up and down the hallway to check on the crystal. When the security guard looked at the crystal, he noticed it looked unusually dark but then suddenly it began to glow brightly. He heard a voice come from the crystal.

It said, "When all worlds unite as one, the king will rise again with the light."

The crystal continued to become brighter and brighter. The light became so bright that the security guard had no choice but to shield his eyes. There was a flash of blinding light, and *poof*, the crystal was gone. The security guard that was on the bench eating his snacks noticed the light and ran back to the hallway to check on the crystal and realized it was gone.

The second security guard exclaimed, "WHAT THE?"

They went to view the camera footage to identify who stole the crystal.

The guy who monitors the cameras yelled, "Hey, you guys! You aren't going to believe this…"

He showed the security guards the footage of the crystal glowing brighter and brighter until it vanished with a flash. They looked at each other puzzled.

The camera guy looked at the security guards and said, "We're out of a job here, aren't we?"

One of the security guards replied, "Looks like it."

The camera guy asked the security guard, "Where do you think the crystal went?"

The security guard shrugged and replied, "Beats me!"

The second security guard chimed in, "We need to contact Rodger and call the police immediately."

*****

Kira was asleep and began to stir because of the presence of extremely bright light. He thought the light was coming from his window. When he opened his eyes, he noticed it wasn't even close to sunrise. When he looked up, he saw the crystal hovering above his bed. He was so surprised he half-jumped/half-fell out of his bed.

He asked, "What's going on? How did this get here? Is that the crystal from the museum?"

The crystal came toward him, and he took a step back, trying to avoid it. Eventually, he couldn't back up any further because his back was against the wall. It kept coming closer. He began to panic.

He yelled, "STOP!"

And the crystal stopped. He noticed it stopped and then he asked it to raise up, then asked it to move down. It did both these things to Kira's amazement. Kira wondered how the crystal came to his house, considering the museum was so far away. He wondered if it teleported and how teleportation would be possible. He heard a voice.

The voice said, "Come…"

He looked around, wondering where the voice came from. He looked back at the crystal and walked closer to it.

He said, "Is the voice coming from you? Are you talking to me? What… I mean, who are you?"

He stretched his hand out toward the crystal, and it flew onto his chest. He tried in vain to pull the crystal off, but he couldn't pull it free. He felt the crystal fuse itself to his body and prepared himself for the pain. His body felt like it was on fire, and it felt extremely painful. When the crystal was fully infused into him, it caused Kira to transform. His skin changed into scales, his nails grew into claws that scratched the wall behind him, his teeth grew into fangs, his hair fell out exposing spikes/horns on his skull, and his eyes changed into those of a dragon's. His feet turned into dragon feet. After he fully transformed, he screamed out in pain/rage which turned into a roar. The roar was so loud it reached Dragza from Earth and the Dark Moon. Revealing to one of the Dragon Knight Warriors (oldest and wisest), Wingsavior, who was meditating until he heard the roar. His eyes shot open and stood up from the floor holding his cane.

He said, "I have found him, the next Dragon King!"

Meanwhile, Dark Strike (leader of the Shadow Dragons) also heard the roar. He opened his eyes and stood up from his throne.

He said, "The time has come. The Core has awakened. Find the source of that roar soldiers."

As they bowed down to Dark Strike, they replied, "As you command, Lord Dark Strike." They vanished into the shadows of the darkness.

Dark Strike said, "And so it begins."

Kira wakes up and thought the whole experience was a weird dream. He couldn't shake the feeling that it was real. He checked his chest for any signs that the crystal had been there then checked the rest of his body. Everything seemed normal. He didn't see anything on his chest and let out a sigh of relief. He let his eyes roll over his reflection in the mirror. He saw his hair changed from blackish-brown to silver on the tips of it. He was so shocked that he stumbled closer to the mirror and knocked his alarm off the nightstand with a crash.

He got really close to the mirror and asked himself, "WHAT HAPPENED? DID I DRINK LAST NIGHT?"

At that moment, his mother called up to him and told him it was time to leave for school, and he can't be late again. He scrambled over to grab his clothes and put them on. He grabbed the door handle, not noticing the large, deep claw marks on the wall behind the door as he ran downstairs, closing the door behind him. He grabbed his breakfast to go and kissed his mom on the cheek. He patted his dad on the back and told him he can't wait to train with him after school. Both of his parents said goodbye and that they love him.

His mom called after him, "When you get home, I'd like to hear about what happened to your other bike, young man!"

Kira grabbed his new bike, turned to his mother, and let out a chuckle, then began to ride his new bike to school. He weaved in and out of alleys and over sidewalks. He got to the same intersection where he was before and slowed down. He saw a group of pedestrians crossing the street. He saw a truck coming down the hill, going way faster than it should. The truck appeared to be speeding up instead of slowing down. It was obvious the truck was out of control. When Kira looked back at the pedestrians who were crossing the street, he noticed a parent and small child who were holding hands. They were walking behind everyone else. They noticed the truck and started to walk a bit faster when the child tripped and her shoe came off. The mom turned to pick the child up, and Kira felt an intense need to save them from getting hurt. When the mom knew it was too late to move out of the way, she tried to shield the child with her body (EVERYTHING GOES INTO SLOW MOTION).

Kira dropped his bike and before he knew what was happening, he ran faster than the speed of light in between them and the truck. He put his hands up to brace himself against the grill of the truck. When the dust settled, it shows that Kira, the mother, and child were not harmed, and the front of the truck was bent upwards with the curve of Kira's hand. The front bumper and engine were absolutely destroyed. Kira slowly opened his eyes as he heard the collective gasp of onlookers. He slowly looked around and released the grill of the truck. He let go of the grill with a *creeeeeeeak* of the metal. He looked at his hands and found them completely undamaged. He looked from his hands to the bumper of the truck in amazement. He turned to check on the mother and her little girl. He found that they were completely unharmed. The mother turned to Kira and thanked him for saving their lives, then turned to check on the child.

Kira was confused about what just happened. He was so shaken that he took off. The driver of the truck came around to the front frantically explaining how his brakes had gone out.

Worried that he hit the mother and child, he shouted, "Are you both all right?"

She replied breathily, "Yes, we're fine."

A crowd had formed, and the first responders rushed in asking what happened and asking how the truck got damaged without causing harm to the pair. The mother told the crowd that a young man stopped the car and saved their lives. When she saw the crowd's confusion, she turned back to look for Kira, but he was already gone. Kira turned back down the alley to hide from the crowd and got off his bike.

He left his bike leaned against the building and thought, *WHAT JUST HAPPENED? THIS ISN'T POSSIBLE! HOW DID I STOP THAT TRUCK WITHOUT GETTING HURT?* He was getting more and more angry with each confusing question.

He yelled, "IT DOESN'T MAKE ANY SENSE!" And punched a hole through bricks of the building.

After a minute of deep breathing, his eyes widened, and he saw the hole he made in the brick wall. He fell back away from the building in horror. He checked his hand expecting to find a broken bone or blood. His hand looked completely normal, not even a scratch. He sat for a moment in amazement, staring from his hand to the hole in the building. He was still trying to process what was happening as he realized that he was going to be late for school AGAIN! With an angry growl, he went to grab his bike and tripped, his hand sliding down the outer wall of the adjacent building. His hand caused claw marks on the wall, and he looked at his hand again, grabbing for the bike handlebars.

"What? I don't have claws," he said, looking at his fingers more closely.

As he did so, he caught the tiniest movement of claws retracting themselves back into his fingers. He shook his head, telling himself that he must be crazy, and he must go to the doctor after school to see why he is hallucinating. He got on his bike, and glancing at his watch, he figured the first bell would be ringing any second. He decided to make his way to school.

"Great. I have claws coming out of my fingers like a werewolf, and Mom's going to kill me," he grumbled to himself, leaving the alleyway.

Kira was completely unaware that the Dragon Knights were watching him from the rooftops as he made his way to school. There were five Dragon Knights clustered on the two rooftops above the alleyway that Kira had just left. One of the Dragon Knights, Rose, stood and contacted Wingsavior through a communication device attached to her wrist.

She said, "We found him."

Wingsavior responded, "Good. I'm glad we finally have."

Rose asked, "Should we go get him?"

Wingsavior said, "Not yet. Just follow him and wait for further instructions. If we found him this easy, the others may not be far behind. Stay vigilant."

Rose answered, "Understood." And turned down the volume on her communicator.

She used Dragzarian hand signals to give instructions to the rest of the team. She instructed two of the Dragon Knights to go follow Kira and keep him safe. She also instructed the other Dragon Knight to go to the museum to check on whether the crystal was still there. She instructed Volt to observe from above with her. They both took flight and hid among the clouds while the other three Dragon Knights quickly began to follow her instructions.

Chapter 5

Kira finally made it to school but realized he had missed his first class completely. After leaving the office, he was on his way to his second class of the day, when he saw the bully, Randall, from yesterday picking on Chuck. Kari was trying to defend him. Chuck made a comment about Randall's beard in spite of Kari's intervention. Randall shoved Kari out of the way and picked Chuck up like he was nothing. She was yelling at Randall to put Chuck down and pounding on his chest. Chuck was scared, and Randall let him drop to the ground.

He turned on Kari, catching her by surprise, and yelled in her face, "Stay out of it!"

She responded, "You're being a jerk to Chuck, and I won't stay out of it."

He was about to punch Kari, and Kira appeared, grabbing his fist before it could hit her. He twisted Randall's arm back painfully.

He told him, "Leave Kari alone."

He pushed Randall away from him. Randall turned and shook off the pain in his arm with a sneer. Randall took in Kira's appearance and recognized him as the same kid from the day before.

He told him, "Make me."

Kira moved his body into a fighting stance, and Randall said, "Oh, okay. You want a beating. Let's have some fun."

Randall snapped his fingers and called the rest of his posse into the circle (five other guys). All six of the guys surrounded Kira, isolating him from Chuck and Kari, who were protesting loudly. Kira looked at each and every one of their faces, keeping himself calm. Kari was shouting at the group to leave Kira alone.

"Oh, we'll leave him alone...once he's in pieces," Randall said with a chuckle.

Kira spoke calmly, saying, "Randall, you don't have to do this. You and your friends can still walk away without getting hurt."

Randall and his friends started laughing loudly.

He said, "You really think you have a chance to take even one of us down?"

Kira smiled in defiance and held his head high, stating, "No. I KNOW I can take you all down."

Randall narrowed his eyes in anger and said, "Oh really?"

Kira nodded, saying, "Give me twenty seconds."

One of the guys behind Kira went to sucker punch him, but he anticipated the punch and dodged it at the last second. The other guys flew into motion, coming at him from all sides. Kira slammed his elbow into the first guy's stomach so hard that the guy cried out and coughed while Kira brought his fist up to break the other guy's nose, causing him to crumple onto the ground. Before anything else could happen, Kira noticed that time slowed to a crawl and then stopped with everyone frozen in place. He looked around and wondered what was going on and why time stopped.

He heard a disembodied voice say, "It stopped because of me."

Kira looked frantically around from side to side to find the source of the voice. "Who said that?"

The voice said, "Up here."

He looked up and saw a floating Golden Warrior in the sky that was shining as bright as the sun. The figure floated down further and further until it touched down onto the ground before Kira.

"Who are you?" Kira asked in amazement.

The figure responded, "I am Leon, King of the Dragons."

Kira responded, "Leon Dragon? You look so familiar…" Kira remembered. "I've envisioned you!"

Leon responded, "Yes, that is true. I tried to warn you about the war that is coming. The war can only be stopped if you fight."

Kira responded, "Me? Unless I fight?"

Leon nodded his golden head and replied, "Yes. The war cannot be won unless you fight. You are the chosen one. The Core chose you to fight in my place."

Kira responded, "The Core? Wait…what Core?"

Leon answered, "The Core takes the form of a crystal in your eyes."

Kira thought back over the events of the last twenty-four hours and realized in amazement that what just happened the night before was definitely not a dream and he had not been hallucinating.

Kira asked, "Why me? Why did the crystal…or Core, choose me? I'm not special…"

Leon responded, "The Core chose you because your heart is pure. You genuinely care for others. You were willing to give your life to save that mother and her child from earlier today."

Kira responded, "You saw that?"

Leon answered, "I see everything."

Kira was quiet for a moment and then asked, "Are you some sort of ghost?"

Leon answered, "I may be a ghost but that does not change the fact that part of my spirit lives within the Core. I am here to guide you to discover the true nature of your powers and to help you become the champion of the light."

Kira said, "You mean like my claws? And how I stopped that truck like it was nothing? Am I?"

Leon finished his sentence by saying, "You…are a Dragzarian. A dragon."

Kira said skeptically, "*Riiiiiiiight*… I'm a dragon…," beginning to doubt his sanity.

Leon stated calmly, "If you don't believe me, see for yourself."

Leon pulled a mirror from his pocket and showed Kira his reflection as a human; he slowly turned the mirror over, and Kira saw his features change into that of a dragon. Kira stumbled backward, clutching his face.

"Is that me? Is that what I look like underneath my skin?"

Leon answered, "Yes, for now. You will have the ability to transform when you need to, but for now, don't worry about transforming. There is a lot to learn before that ability. One day, you will be a champion."

Kira calmed down a bit and took a few deep breaths. "Okay, so say, I believe you and"—he gestured around him—"all this. How do I become a champion?"

Leon smiled and said, "That is for another time, my son."

Kira took a moment to think and said, "Okay. What am I supposed to do with them? How do I handle all this?" he asked, pointing to Randall and his crew frozen in time.

Leon answered calmly placing his hand/claw on Kira's shoulder. "Trust your instincts, as a Dragon and as a warrior. They will never lead you astray. Unleash the Dragon Spirit from inside you."

Kira closed his eyes and slowly focused on his breathing. He felt his heart pulse faster and faster. When his eyes opened, they had morphed into the eyes of a dragon. Time came rushing back in a flash, whirling everything into motion.

The other four guys came at him with angry roars with Kira standing in the middle of their circle. At the last moment before their fists would have touched him, Kira vanished silently, causing the four to throw punches at each other, not noticing his disappearance in the chaos. When the guys realized he disappeared, their confusion turned to anger. They were nursing their faces and bruises.

Kira yelled, "HEY!" And turned their attention back to him.

"Looking for someone?"

Each of the guys started to rush at Kira.

Kari was yelling, "WATCH OUT!"

He closed his eyes and took four deep breaths, and everything slowed down around him again. He opened his senses and found he could sense everything, from the beads of sweat falling from Randall's temple to a spider crawling up its web on the school building. When a guy got close to him, he opened his eyes and did a judo flip and threw him into a dumpster. Two of the guys were about to punch him from either side, but Kira did a side flip causing the two to hit each other instead. One punch went into a guy's groin and the other hit in the stomach. Kira did a handstand and turned it into a split kick without hesitation. He landed with surprise because he executed the kick flawlessly. Another guy tried to hit him, and he dodged all the punches. Another tried to charge at him. He hit the first guy in the elbow and did a backflip, causing the two to run into each other head-on and knock each other out. While Kira was lost in his amazement, one of the guys grabbed a bat and was about to swing to hit him in the back.

Kari and Chuck screamed, "WATCH OUT BEHIND YOU!"

Kira blocked the bat with his forearm, breaking and splintering the wood where it struck his skin. Kira checked his arm for injuries and found none. The guy gasped in amazement, and Kira made a fist at him with his raised arm. The guy dropped his bat and ran away. Kira looked back at his arm and heard Leon's voice saying that this lack of injury was one of his people's powers. Leon told him that more information would come later, but now he must focus on the fight at hand.

Kira turned and found Randall advancing with brass knuckles. He did a fast turn move and blocked the fist. Randall then tried to hit him with the other fist, and Kira blocked that one too. Randall began to growl at him in anger. Kira growled back, but the sound was not a human growl. Kira's eyes changed to dragon eyes. Randall got scared when he noticed the changes.

Randall said, "What are you?"

Kira broke both of Randall's wrists, who screamed, and his eyes rolled back before he passed out. Kira was holding Randall up to do more damage, but Mia shouted at him, telling him to stop. His eyes changed back to human eyes, and he laid Randall down gently on the ground. He looked over at Kari, Chuck, and the rest of the onlookers, which included Mia, his little sister. Kira looked down at his hands in horror at what he had done and the anger he showed. He was afraid of what he would have done if Mia hadn't stopped him.

Chuck came toward him, telling him, "That was amazingly awesome!"

Kira turned and ran away. Chuck and Kari exchanged looks and out of concern, ran after him to check on him.

On the rooftop of the school, Rose and her troops observed the fight from above.

Rose told her troops, "There is no denying that he is the one we are looking for…"

They could all sense an unusual power in Kira. They could sense that his power was growing exponentially. One of the troops suggested that they retrieve him now, but Rose disagreed and stated they must follow the orders from Wingsavior.

She said, "Wingsavior told us to keep an eye on him, and THAT's what we're going to DO."

The others began chattering about what would happen if the Shadow Dragons found him or them first.

Rose said with a confident smile, "Their technology is way slower than ours. They won't find him for weeks if ever. IF, and that's a big IF, they find him, then we do what we always do best, we fight."

The group then flew into the air to hide from any human's view.

Kira rode his bike fast all the way back to his house, throwing it down on the lawn and rushing inside. Ignoring his parents' questions and surprise, he ran upstairs to his room and slammed the door. His mother and father exchanged glances and began to discuss how they should handle the situation.

Soon after, Mia came home from school and explained what happened during the fight to her parents. Chuck and Kari arrived soon after Mia and spoke to Kira's parents. After they learned what happened, his father went upstairs to speak with him as father and son. He knocked gently on the door and Kira did not respond. His father asked if he could come in and Kira said sure. Kira asked him if he knew what happened, and his father told him yes. Kira was about to explain and apologize for what happened.

His father raised his palm and said, "Don't. It's true you may have been angry enough to kill him, but you didn't. You let him go. You have a right to protect your loved ones. Another fight like that could land you in real trouble."

Kira shook his head in understanding and said, "I know."

His dad patted him on the shoulder and said, "I'm proud of you for standing up for your friends and what you believe in, son."

Kira was shocked and raised his head to look at his dad. Kira asked, "Really?"

His father nodded and broke into a smile. "Yes."

Kira's eyes filled with unshed tears, and he said, "Thank you for understanding."

His dad smiled wider and said, "Hey, I'm your dad. I always understand."

Kira puts out his hand for a handshake, and his father moved the hand away and pulled him into a bear hug.

Kira's father said, "No matter what happens, no matter what you become, even a warrior, you'll always be my son. Your mother and I will always love you."

Kira said, "What about Mia?"

Kira's father chuckled and said, "Yeah, her too."

Kira laughed. His door opened and his mother, Mia, Kari, and Chuck crowded in.

He hastily wiped the unshed tears away, smiling, and said, "Hey."

Kira's mom came in and put her arms around him, causing Mia and Kari to hug him too. Once they were done hugging, Chuck came up and offered his fist for a "fist bump." Kira's mom suggested that since they were all there, they should go out to dinner as a family, with Chuck and Kari too. Kira's mom, Mia, Kari, and Chuck shuffled out of Kira's room to go back downstairs.

Kira's father turned and got up off the bed, asking, "Are you coming, son?"

Kira nodded and said, "Yeah. I just need a minute." (As he looked at the claw marks on his wall).

His father patted his shoulder and said, "Okay. See you downstairs." He then left the room.

Kira shuffled around his room for a moment and bent to pick up his jacket. He caught a glimpse of himself in the mirror. He saw a dragon, which reflected that of Leon Dragon.

Leon said, "You are lucky to have a good family and good friends." He explained that he understands why the Spirit Core chose him. He continues, "Now that I know why you were chosen, I'll be looking forward to working alongside you, in body and spirit. If you ever need me, let me know." His reflection vanished, revealing a reflection of Kira underneath.

He went downstairs, a bit shaken up, to catch up with the others. They all went out for dinner.

Throughout dinner, the family was watched by the pack of Shadow Dragons disguised as humans. They can use their eyes to sense power/auras and were using them to locate the powerful one. They used their abilities and found that Kira was the one they were searching for. The lieutenant pointed at Kira and indicated he is the one. One of the other Shadow Dragons made a move to go toward him and the lieutenant stuck out his arm to stop him.

He said, "Not yet! First, we must make sure the Dragon Knights are not here too. Plus, there are too many people in the way. We have to wait for the right moment...a moment when he is alone..."

One of the comrades stated, "How do we get him without them knowing?"

The lieutenant responded, "Just leave that to me!"

Around eight o'clock, once everyone had played every game twice, the family headed home. They dropped off Kari and Chuck at their place. The two of them wished Kira good luck in the tournament the next morning (Saturday). He thanked them shyly. The family continued home without noticing that the Shadow Dragons were following them. They finally arrived back home, and everyone filed into the house.

The legion of Shadow Dragons watched with rapt attention as the family moved inside. They were hiding in the shadows, knowing that the Dragon Knights were there too. The lieutenant realized they needed to wait for the Dragon Knights to be called away. Their plan was for all the Shadow Dragons on Dragza to start a full-scale assault. With a big battle raging on Dragza, the lieutenant knew the Dragon Knights would have to return there to fight. It was very important that the Shadow Dragons stay hidden until the Dragon Knights were called away. They left Kira unattended, thinking that he was safe, and they were nowhere around. As they were watching and waiting, the impatient one rushed forward toward the nearest house. The lieutenant snatched him back so forcefully that he slammed into the outer wall of the nearest house with a grunt.

"NOT YET," the lieutenant whisper-yelled at the bruised dragon, grabbing him by the throat. "I TOLD YOU TO WAIT! BE PATIENT!" he hissed.

The dragon asked angrily, "So when do we attack?" Shrugging off the lieutenant's hand.

The lieutenant sighed with attitude and said, "I don't usually share my plans with the likes of you, but I'll make an exception in this case before you get us all killed. First, the Dragon Knights will be returning to Dragza shortly... Two, we overheard the boy discuss a tournament tomorrow, correct?"

The disobedient dragon nodded.

"Well, while he's at this tournament, we will put a little plan in place of our own. It seems as though the boy may come quietly if we take the three very special people in his life..." The lieutenant finished, turning his attention back to the house with an evil grin.

All the Shadow Dragons began to slip back into the darkness unnoticed. Except for one Shadow Dragon, who hid behind a bush. The lieutenant glared in his direction, coming forward more into the light.

He grabbed the bush-hiding dragon by the scruff of his neck and whispered, "Come on!"

Later that evening, Rose called together the dragon troops that were watching over Kira.

She explained, "The Shadow Dragons have started an all-out attack on Dragza. Wingsavior needs us to return to get the situation under control."

One of the Dragon Knights piped in saying, "Are you sure that's a good idea, to leave the boy alone like that?"

Rose replied, "We have to trust that the crystal has chosen wisely."

The Dragon Knights left and returned to Dragza.

"Just as I planned," the lieutenant exclaimed with an evil chuckle.

*****

The first glimpse is the outside of the arena. Kira's entire family attended together. In attendance were the Shadow Dragons, who were either disguised as humans or up in the rafters/lights. They watched all the rounds. Kira's first opponent was a guy that was bigger/more muscular than him.

Both he and his opponent bowed to one another, and Kira said, "May the best fighter win."

When his opponent went to punch him, Kira moved so quickly, it looked like he disappeared. The opponent was confused.

And Kira yelled, "Want to try again?"

The opponent growled and went for him. Kira dodged and blocked every one of his moves.

During his opponent's last punch, Kira grabbed his fist and said, "My turn."

The opponent's eyebrows squinted, and one went up in confusion. Kira landed a strong punch in his stomach. After his opponent had recovered from the punch, he did a flip somersaulting in the air. He then did the iron fist technique, hitting the opponent so hard that he was pushed out of the ring and sprawled on the ground. This caused the entire crowd to go silent because they weren't sure if Kira's opponent was alive.

Kira yelled to him, asking, "Hey, you okay?"

The opponent slowly got to his feet, and the audience began to clap with Kira's family clapping a bit. The Shadow Dragons plus other crowd members were blown away by how strong and trained he seemed. The opponent and Kira made a vow to remain respectful toward one another. There was a montage of Kira facing all the other opponents one by one. It ends with the final opponent and Kira's victory. It shows Kira's family standing and cheering in the audience at his first-place victory.

Chapter 6

The family headed back home together, excitedly chattering about the competition. Once they got home, Kira rushed upstairs to put his trophy down. His father followed him and asked him where he learned the Dragon Style and all the others he exhibited. Kira told him that he had no idea. The moves came to him when he was dreaming. His father was amazed but not completely convinced. He decided he would keep a closer eye on Kira to make sure everything was okay. He told him how proud he was and how much he loved him.

After dinner, everyone went to bed, especially Kira because he was so exhausted. Just before he fell asleep, his cell phone began to ring. At first, he decided not to answer it but changed his mind.

When he said hello, the caller responded, "Hey bro! It's been a long time since we've seen each other. The last time at summer camp!"

Realizing who the voice belonged to on the other end, Kira jumped up from his bed knowing it was his long-lost friend, Jack.

With new-awakened energy and excited tone, Kira shouted, "Jack? Hey man! How've you been, bro?"

Jack responded, "Been doing good, bro! I heard on the news about your tournament win and congrats!"

Kira responded, "Hey, thanks, dude! That means a lot coming from you! Let's get together to catch up on things!"

Jack exclaimed, "Let's meet up tomorrow at Crossroads Café about 2:00 p.m."

Kira, in a most-excited voice, said, "Sure thing! Can't wait to see you there, bro!"

They both said good night and Kira laid back down for a pleasant, much-needed rest. Kira went to sleep thinking about Leon. He wondered if all the moves he exhibited were from Leon, or if any of that was really him. Leon acknowledged that it came from Kira, but the ability came from the Spirit Core. The Core increased his balance and flexibility and overall physical strength and abilities. They spoke for a few more moments before Kira turned to exit the dream world.

Leon grasped his shoulder gravely and said, "Be forewarned. Those who seek you will come near, and they might be either friend or foe. But only time will tell."

He began to fade away, leaving Kira with a sick feeling of dread. "Huh? Who? When will they come?"

Leon responded, "You'll know soon enough. Beware! Their actions will not only affect your life, but all those you love as well…"

Kira shouted, "Wait! What does that mean?"

Kira then woke up in a cold sweat.

After Kira was awake, he sat up quickly and looked around the room. He saw everything was just as he left it. He swiped his hand across his forehead, wondering what Leon was warning him about. He tried to think about what Leon's warning could mean, but he couldn't wrap his sleepy head around it. He settled back into his bed and tried to go back to sleep.

After a few moments, his eyes shot back open, and he checked the clock. If he didn't wake up now, he would be late to visit with his old friend Jack at the Crossroads Cafe. They met at a summer camp when they were children and hadn't seen each other in about ten years. After the tournament, there was a news article about Kira and the trophy. Jack saw Kira's picture and recognized him (Jack had a picture of the two of them from camp, and Kira's appearance hadn't changed). Jack tracked him down and wanted to reconnect.

When Jack arrives at the coffee shop, he sees Kira sitting alone at a table, stirring his coffee. Kira had been waiting there patiently for about an hour. When the two saw each other, they clasped hands in delight and appreciation. Kira stood up and Jack patted him on the shoulder. They both sat down at the table and began to catch up on everything that happened over the last ten years. Jack began to tell Kira about the work he had been doing in the family's business of robotics. Kira asked Jack how he knew about the tournament. He said because he saw him on TV, and that's the reason he found him again. Jack asked about why the tips of his hair were silver and if he had dyed it.

Kira pushed his hair around and said, "You could say that…"

Jack arched an eyebrow, and Kira mumbled that he would explain later. Jack nodded and changed the subject by inviting Kira over to hang out at the mansion whenever he's free. Kira asked if it would be okay if he brought a few guests over with him (like his family and friends). Jack nodded and responded that he could bring anyone he wanted if they weren't annoying.

Kira laughed and said, "Fair enough."

The two stood and shook hands affectionately. They exchanged addresses and both promised to keep in touch.

Kira was walking back to his house when he saw several rescue vehicles pass him headed in that direction. He began to walk faster and noticed that there was a huge crowd surrounding his house. He ran up the steps and ducked under a caution tape. A gruff policeman put a hand on his shoulder and asked him what he was doing.

Kira shook off his hand and said, "This is my house!"

The policeman responded, "You don't want to go in there, son!"

Kira pushed past him and went inside the living room anyway. He saw all the curtains ripped up, furniture destroyed, and everything strewn all over. He saw the remnants of his trophy scattered all over the room and some walls covered in blood. There were people drawing chalk lines around a man's body in the corner, and when he got closer, he discovered that it was his father. In the hallway, his mother was being worked on by a medical team. Her arm had been severed from her body, and she was losing a lot of blood. She was still breathing, and all Kira could hear was her crying.

He ran over to her and started yelling, "Mom! Mom!"

She opened her eyes and looked at him unfocused. She said, "Kira?"

He kissed her forehead, and she used her remaining arm to catch his head before he could pull away. She whispered what happened into his ear.

A group had come searching for Kira. They pounded on the door and demanded him to come out. Kira's father told them he wasn't there and to leave him alone. He told them if they didn't leave, he would call the police. They broke the door off its hinges and rushed in. The noise attracted Kira's mom and Mia, and they both came into the living room. Kira's mom screamed for Mia to run and get out of there quickly. She picked up the phone to call 911. Kira's dad was trying to fight off the group of creatures, but his karate was no match for their powers. He took a few down with his kicks and punches, and just as he was about to kick another, one of them shot him in the heart with a finger blast. Kira's mom screamed in terror and picked up anything in sight she could find to fight them off with. The creatures tried asking her where Kira was and when he'd be home, but she wouldn't do anything but cry and fight. Two of the creatures went after Mia, and Kira's mother tried frantically to fight them off. She got a few good hits in, but when she tried to put more force into her punches, one of the creatures ripped off her arm and tossed her against the wall. They glanced around the house and decided that this way of doing things wasn't getting them anywhere. They decided they would kidnap Mia instead.

Kira was openly crying now as his mom started to repeat the phrase, "We love you, Kira. Please find your sister."

Kira began to ask her, "Where is she? Where is Mia?"

With her last breath, her hand slipped down off his neck and fell to the gurney. Her eyes went misty, and he couldn't feel her pulse anymore. There was a call to action by the medical staff, and his mother's gurney was pushed away from him without haste. The medics tried to work on her, and after a few minutes, they shook their heads and gave the time of death. Kira was in shock, but he knew he had to find his sister. He ran upstairs to Mia's room and found it had also been destroyed. He found a note secured onto her bed with a knife. He pulled the knife out carefully and bent to read the note. The note reads: "If you EVER want to see your sister alive again, meet us at the abandoned mall. Come alone. Otherwise, she will die worse than your parents." Kira's hands crushed the paper in anger. He tucked the knife into his waistband and climbed out the window.

Stealthily avoiding the police, he grabbed his bike and rushed off to the mall.

Kira pulled up to the mall and hid his bike in a place where it wouldn't be seen. He snuck silently into the mall. The group of Shadow Dragons was waiting for him to arrive. One was sharpening a stick with his claws while the other creature was pacing back and forth. The lieutenant sat with Mia while she steadily sobbed quietly. The lieutenant told Mia there was nothing to be afraid of because all they wanted was Kira. Once they had him, they'd let her go.

Mia dried her eyes somewhat and asked, "What do you want with my brother?"

The lieutenant explained, "Kira has something we want, and we plan on getting it back."

One of the privates chipped in, saying, "Yeah, even if we have to rip out his heart to get it."

All the other creatures laughed, except for the lieutenant, who gave that private a glare. Mia began crying again and yelled at them to leave Kira alone. She was screaming so much that the lieutenant rolled his eyes and backhanded her. She hit the ground, and the lieutenant pulled out his knife and pointed it at her.

"Who died and made you my commander? The only leader who can tell us what to do is Lord Dark Strike. If you dare try to command us again, I will cut you with this knife."

Mia glared at the lieutenant rebelliously, and he made a move to bring the knife closer to her throat.

Kira's voice was heard over the loudspeaker, "Leave my sister alone!"

Mia shouted out, "Kira," breaking into a smile. The lieutenant scooped Mia up in his arms and held the knife against her throat, glancing around, trying to find Kira in the shadows. Kira suddenly revealed himself.

Noticing Kira, the lieutenant said, "So you finally came…"

Kira responded, "I only came to give this back…" He threw the knife directly at the lieutenant, causing him to pull Mia and himself out of the way.

The knife caught one of the other creatures in the chest. The private pulled it out slowly and his skin healed instantly.

The lieutenant jumped up and told the rest of his squad, "Boys, let's have a little fun."

Kira was able to block a few of the blows but was sucker punched by one of the privates and fell to the ground. The three privates began to punch and kick him for the lieutenant's amusement. Mia cried softly and looked away from Kira, glancing at her purse. She remembered that she still had the Taser inside it and began to plan on how to use it to help them survive.

Kira thought to himself, *How can I save Mia? How can I get us out of this?* He began to call out in his mind for Leon. He thought, *Leon, if you can hear me, I need you now!* He even shouted out Leon's name.

Kira's eyes opened, and it shows that time stood still as he went back into the dream world to meet with Leon.

Leon said, "I am here to provide you with guidance. You did not heed my warning, and I am not sure if you're ready. But I will help you through this crisis. I know you want to defeat them. To do this, we need to unleash the power."

Kira was confused and asked how.

Leon explained, "To unleash the power, you must clear your mind and let the Spirit take over. You must repeat these words: Awaken the Dragon."

Kira began to repeat the phrase over and over again. Outside his mind, one of the creatures was about to sucker punch him, and Mia made her move with the taser. She tased the lieutenant and the move backfired. The taser blew up, throwing Mia against the wall (knocking her unconscious) and the lieutenant across the room. He got to his feet and stooped to pick up a sledgehammer.

"I've had enough of this..." He walked over to Kira and said, "Say goodnight, maggot."

As he swung the hammer down to crush his chest, Kira's hand shot up and stopped the hammer. Kira began pushing up off the ground, and the lieutenant was bewildered. Kira's body was glowing, and his eyes opened. His eyes were glowing as well, and his clothes moved in an unseen wind.

He grabbed the sledgehammer away and said, "Good night, you monster."

He used the sledgehammer to smack the lieutenant away.

As a final touch, Kira yelled, "Awaken the dragon!"

And a burst of light exploded from his body, crashing into the other creatures and making them all fall over.

Chapter 7

The explosion shook the building, and the room filled with dust and smoke. Mia began to stir, regaining consciousness. She slowly got up from the ground but couldn't see anything because of the smoke. She saw the creatures on the ground also beginning to get up. They were shaking their heads, and the lieutenant pushed himself out of the rubble of the wall. They all looked toward the center of the room where a figure was silhouetted. The figure was on its knees in the center of the room. They assumed that the figure was Kira and began to surround it.

As the smoke began to clear, the figure was revealed to be someone else entirely. It began to rise to its feet, and the figure's body becomes front and center. They thought they knew who the figure was. It shows the figure dressed in armor as a warrior would be, and it is revealed that the figure is that of Kira, only he had transformed. He pulled out his hands and began to assess the changes in his body composition and attire. He realized that this must be the power that Leon said would save his sister's life. He began to speak to Kira in his head and confirmed that this is the power he had mentioned. He explained that Kira had unleashed the power of a true dragon, and he alone can defeat the Shadow Dragons. He goes on to state that from this day on, he is no longer known as Kira Scott. He is now Strike Dragon.

After Strike finished speaking to Leon, he whispered, "Strike Dragon," over and over.

One of the creatures pointed to Strike and yelled in terror, "That's Leon! That's Leon DRAGON!"

The lieutenant smacked the creature in the face, yelling, "You idiot! That's not Leon Dragon! That's the boy!" The lieutenant pointed to Strike and said, "His skin is silver!"

39

The creature took another look at Strike and said, "Hey! Yeah! That's not Leon!"

Strike looks at the creatures with a serious expression.

The lieutenant shouted, "GET HIM!"

The creatures jumped into the air, ready to fight.

After they were on their feet, Strike cracked his knuckles and said to himself, "All right. It's showtime!"

One by one, they attacked him. One tried to hit him with a left hook, another tried a right. One tried to slash him with his claws, and another tried to kick with a spin. He avoided all their blows as though he knew they were coming. He stood in the center of the creatures, uninjured, and they gasped at him in disbelief that he wasn't hurt. Not one scratch. He bent his four fingers in a gesture, signaling for the creatures to come get him. One of them was annoyed with him at this point and charged at him full force. The creature raised both of his fists to bash Strike (a move called the sledgehammer). Strike easily caught the creature's hands in one of his claws. The creature snarled in anger, and Strike raised his other hand, wiggling his forefinger back and forth in his face, making a small "*tsk, tsk*" sound. Strike slowly made a fist with his upraised hand and began to glow with cosmic energy.

He looked directly into his opponent's eyes and said, "My turn."

He sent a shockwave that sent the creature flying to the air, right through the roof of the abandoned mall. The creature landed in a body of water located several miles away.

Strike looked at the remaining creatures and said menacingly, "Who's next?"

One of the creatures pulled out a knife and charged. Strike pulled one of the swords from his back and did a backflip, causing the creature to miss his mark. He landed on his feet with his back toward the creature with the knife. The creature staggered, and Strike put his sword back into its sheath, showing the creature behind him split into two halves.

The lieutenant shouted, "That's not possible!"

The remaining two, instead of attacking him one at a time, decided to attack together. They began to circle around him. They both tried to attack at once. One sent a punch and the other sent a kick, which Strike blocked. This began a fast-paced fighting sequence. The lieutenant was amazed at the boy's movements and speed. He then had a vision of a past fight when he had fought with Leon. He thought that Strike may be the next Dragon King after all.

Strike continued to block every hit thrown at him. He seized an opportunity to exit the fight as both creatures came in for big hits. One, a left hook and another for a kick. As Strike moved, they ended up hitting each other and began to argue.

Strike yelled to them and said, "Hey! Are we going to fight, or do you want to just keep arguing?"

The two glanced at each other then looked back at Strike.

One said, "Shall we?" And the other nodded.

They both charged at Strike. Strike used an energy burst again to smack one of them through a wall. There was a sharp object on the other side, which impelled the creature, killing him instantly. Strike continued to dodge the other enraged creature's punches until he was able to grab a hold of the creature's head. He smashed its skull on the ground then delivered a final kick to the creature, which created a huge crater in the ground. Out of nowhere, the creature who was thrown from the mall returned and tried to execute a sneak attack on him, but with a quick reflex, Strike turned and fired a beam of energy from his hand, vaporizing the creature along with a large portion of the mall, causing the building to shudder and become unstable.

Strike turned back toward the lieutenant. He held Mia in his arms and backed up further and further. He warned Strike that he needed to stay back, or he would kill the girl. The lieutenant shook with dread as he looked into Strike's eyes. Strike rushed on him fast, snatching his knife and pushing Mia out of the way and pinning the lieutenant to the wall.

Strike said, "No. You won't."

Strike wrapped his fingers around the lieutenant's throat, and the lieutenant begged for mercy, saying, "Please."

Strike said, "Did you show my parents mercy?" He smashed his head against the wall. "DID YOU?" He smashed the lieutenant's head against the wall again.

The lieutenant panicked and said, "I had no choice! I was ordered!"

Strike came really close to his face and said, "Who! Who sent you?"

The lieutenant shut his mouth in fear and shook his head defiantly. To show his frustration and his resolve, Strike punched the wall right next to the lieutenant's head and left a huge crater.

Strike screamed, "WHO? ANSWER ME!"

The entire mall shook with his words.

The lieutenant closed his eyes in defeat and said in a small voice, "His name is… Dark Strike. We got our orders from him."

Strike raised his hand and drew out his claws, ready to stab him in the heart.

The lieutenant screamed, "No! PLEASE NO, *NOOOOO*!"

Mia jumped up and began calling out to Strike, sobbing. She appealed to him by calling him Kira.

She said, "No, Kira! Please!"

Strike turned back to glare at her, and when he saw her tear-streaked eyes, his heart broke for her. His eyes turned back to normal, and his claws retracted.

He said her name sadly, "Mia."

He let go of the lieutenant and let him sink to the floor. He enveloped Mia in his arms and apologized, saying that he didn't mean to scare her. After a moment, the lieutenant struggled to his feet. Strike noticed and gently let go of Mia. He glared coldly at the lieutenant and walked toward him. The lieutenant flinched and waited for a blow to come, but it never did.

Instead, Strike leaned in real close and whispered, "Do not be fooled. You are alive because of her," he said pointing at Mia. "If I ever see the likes of you again, she will not be there to stop me next time. Understood?" Strike hissed.

The lieutenant nodded slowly and made a move.

Strike pushed him back with a hand on his chest. "You take this message to Dark Strike. Tell him that Strike Dragon is coming for him."

The lieutenant nodded eagerly.

After a moment, Strike moved his hand, and the lieutenant ran for the exit, not stopping to collect any of his weapons. Strike watched him flee then made his way back to Mia. He picked her up in his arms and carried her out of the mall to find a safe place. The two of them started to grieve losing their parents all over again. As Strike walked outside with Mia, he was engrossed in his own thoughts.

After a few minutes, he noticed that he wasn't walking. He was *floating*. He began to get nervous and then Leon began to speak to him once more. Leon told him that Dragzarians can fly, with or without wings. Leon said that flight depended on the amount of Dragoon Energy, it is something a Dragzarian possesses.

Strike said, "I see it now."

Mia turned from his chest and looked up at him and asked, "What?" She noticed how far they were above Earth and began to freak out.

Strike calmed her down, stating that he can fly, and she need not worry. Mia asked how all this happened and how any of this was possible.

Strike looked down at her and said, "It's kind of a long story."

He thought about where he should take Mia where she would be safe. He decided to take her to Jack's mansion. As quickly as he thought it, they were there.

Strike landed on the ground with a little help from Leon. He sat Mia next to the door, and he rang the doorbell. Mia asked him if he should be ringing the doorbell because he still looks like a dragon. He was about to respond when the butler opened the door.

The butler said, "How may I help you?"

Strike had already miraculously transformed back into Kira.

Kira turned to the butler and said, "Uh, yeah…is Jack home?"

Kira and Mia were escorted around the mansion by the butler. He led the pair down to Jack's gym where he was practicing punching techniques with a partner. The butler announced that Jack's friends, Kira and Mia, had arrived. Jack turned and looked.

He said, "Ah… Kira! Glad you could make it!"

Jack's sparring partner was about to deliver a punch, but Jack blocked it without looking, delivering an uppercut to his sparring partner's jaw, which caused him to fly up in the air, and the bell dinged. Jack offered his partner a hand to help him up.

Jack patted the man's shoulder and muttered, "Let's take a break. You've earned it."

Jack began taking off his equipment and walking down the stairs from the ring. Jack and Kira walked toward each other, briefly grasping hands in greeting.

Kira told Jack, "You still got it!"

Jack said with a chuckle, "Just like old times."

Kira said smiling, "Just like old times."

Mia gave a fake cough to remind Kira that she was still there and hadn't been introduced. Kira glanced back at her, remembering that she was there.

"Oops. Almost forgot. Jack, this is my sister, Mia. Mia, this is my friend, Jack."

They shook hands and exchanged greetings.

Jack changed the subject and asked, "So not that I mind, but what brings you two all the way out here?"

Kira explained that the two of them could really use a safe place to stay. Jack told them they were always welcome there. After that, they all settled down and started to relax. They settled in and Jack got them both something to drink. Kira started explaining to Jack the whole story about his parents the best he could. He told Jack how the creatures who killed them had kidnapped Mia and how he fought to get her back. Kira left out the part about him transforming into a dragon. Jack was shocked and asked why they would do such a thing.

He asked, "Why would they kill your parents and kidnap Mia? It's almost as if they want something from you, Kira."

Mia, piping up, said, "It has to be something they want *from Kira. I don't know what it is*, but I think it has something to do with what he is…" Mia looked at Kira expectantly.

Jack was confused and said, "Come again?"

Kira took a few breaths and said, "It'll be easier to show you than to try to explain…"

Jack nodded and waited.

Kira took a step back and after a few moments, he said, "Awaken the Dragon."

At first, nothing happened. Kira was confused and tried to figure out why nothing was happening. He decided to try again.

He said, "AWAKEN THE DRAGON," as he had said it earlier in the day.

All of a sudden, there was a blinding bright light. Mia and Jack couldn't see anything and had to shield their eyes. When the bright light faded, Jack was able to look where Kira once stood. When Jack looked, his jaw dropped. He saw a dragon-like man standing where Kira had been a moment before. Jack gasped in amazement.

"K-Kira? Is that you?"

Strike nodded and said, "Yes. But in this form, I am called Strike Dragon."

Jack walked up to Strike and patted his shoulder. Jack needed to see if what he was seeing was real.

He said, "Good to know you..." and then Jack abruptly passed out.

Strike looked at Mia and said, "Was it something I said?"

They both began to chuckle.

Mia and Strike picked Jack up and put him down gently on the couch. After a while, Jack came to, and Mia's face was all he could see.

Jack slowly sat up and muttered, "What happened?"

Strike popped over and said, "Glad you're up!" Which gave Jack a scare.

After a few moments, everything sank in for Jack, and he started being excited about what Kira's transformation could mean.

Jack put two and two together and said, "KIRA! You can be a superhero!"

Mia agreed, and Strike began to ponder.

He thought out loud, saying, "But in order to use these powers, I would need lots of practice. Somewhere that I can keep my identity secret."

Jack jumped up and said triumphantly, "I think I can help you with that, but I'll need a couple of weeks to get everything ready..."

Strike nodded at him and said, "Thanks, I appreciate it."

Mia, looking from Strike to Jack and wrapping her arms around herself, asked nervously, "Where do we live? What do we do?"

Strike dropped his head in sadness, remembering that they no longer had a home or parents to take care of them.

Jack thought for a moment and said, "Let me talk to my dad and see if you can stay with us for a while. He really liked your parents, and I'm sure he wouldn't mind too much. I might even be able to get you into my school…"

Strike shook his head and said, "It's too much to ask. I can't ask you to—"

Jack clasped his shoulder and said, "Dude. It's the least I can do. You just lost your parents. Let me help." He glanced at Mia, who was still holding herself. "Let me help both of you."

Strike was silent for a moment and was about to speak when Mia interrupted. "I don't want to change schools. I like our school. I like my friends. I don't want anything else to change," she said, tears starting to run down her face.

Jack nodded in acceptance and went to call his father. Mia looked at Strike, and he came over and wrapped her up in a fierce hug, letting a few tears stream down his face.

Chapter 8

The next few weeks for Kira and Mia were a blur. Meetings with social workers, policemen, grief counselors, and lawyers filled their after-school hours. Jack's father was able to get temporary custody of the two of them until another solution could be found or other relatives come forward. During this time, Kira cut himself off from everyone, especially Chuck and Kari, who were very worried about him. Kira would barely talk to them during breaks and would disappear during lunch. He missed a lot of days, preferring to practice his skills in the abandoned mall and not being able to focus in school. Mia threw herself into her schoolwork, trying to distract herself from how much she missed her parents. The family home was cleaned after the police finished with it, and Kira and Mia were able to move a lot of their stuff over to Jack's house. The family house sat waiting for a decision to be made about its future.

On the last day of school, June 10, 2015, Chuck and Kari decided that Kira wouldn't avoid them on that day. There was going to be an assembly for all students to meet and exchange yearbooks. Chuck and Kari left the gymnasium and found Kira in his favorite place on campus, under the biggest willow on campus, trying to meditate. In happier times, the three of them would spend their lunches together under that tree, but today Kira sat alone, eyes closed in concentration. Kari and Chuck exchanged worried looks.

Kari was about to say Kira's name to let him know that they were there, but before she did, Kira's eyes flashed open, and he caught her wrist. Startled, Kari gasped and Kira, noticing who she was, immediately dropped his hand.

Face scrunched up in guilt and flushed from the surprise, Kira said, "Kari, you scared the crap outa me, and I'm sorry I reacted the way I did. Is your wrist okay?"

Kari's heart began to slow, and she then rubbed gently on her wrist.

Sitting down close to Kira, she said, "My wrist will be okay. Kira…we're really worried about you…"

Chuck recovered from his surprise at Kira's movement and sat in the corner opposite Kari, closing the triangle.

"Yeah, man. We haven't seen you in ages. It's only been a month since your parents…"

At the mention of his parents, Kira's face hardened, and he looked away, clenching his fists at the pain in his heart. Kari shot Chuck a look, shaking her head as a signal for him to drop the subject.

Mid-sentence, Chuck changed the trajectory and finished with, "We just want you to know that we are here for you. For whatever you need…"

She let out the breath she was holding and added, "You and Mia can even stay with me over the summer. I've already talked to my parents about it… Well…it was actually my mom's idea even…" Kari kept rambling for a few seconds, and Kira stood up silently.

He looked at each of his friends' faces, at a loss for what to say and not able to open up about everything just yet, considering Kari and Chuck don't know everything about his powers or his parents' deaths. Kira closed his eyes for a moment and took a deep breath.

"Guys," he said sadly, "I'm sorry I haven't been talking to you lately. There's just too much happening right now. I'm not ready to talk about it. I'm not ready to…" Kira's eyes filled with unshed tears. "I'm not ready to accept that they're gone."

Chuck and Kari nodded in understanding, and Kari reached out to hug him.

Kira moved out of her reach and said, "Mia and I already have somewhere to stay this summer. I just…need space."

Chuck asked, "Space from what?"

Kira looked at the ground and said, "From everything."

Chuck continued, "Even from us?"

He responded, "Especially from you." Pushing past both of them, he mumbled, "I'm sorry," under his breath, barely louder than a whisper.

Once out from below the tree, he took off as fast as he could, trying to be anywhere but there. Chuck and Kari's faces both reflected some pain, like Kira's words had injured them. Kari had a tear slip down her cheek, and Chuck pulled her into a hug.

"Was it something I did?" she asked into Chuck's shoulder.

He shook his head. "No, Kari. He isn't himself right now. He knows we will be here when he needs us. Just not right now."

The two friends shared a long hug, and afterward, they made their way back to the assembly, sadder than they were before. Kira found himself on the other side of the school in seconds. He began to take out his frustration on boulders in the front of the school, feeling guilty for what he felt and for what he had just said to his best friends. He felt completely and utterly alone in the world for the first time in his life.

After a few weeks of restless days and haunting nights, the facility Jack talked about was finally ready. Jack took Kira and Mia to a secret room underground.

The room was completely dark until Jack said, "Power on," which turned on the entire room.

The lights revealed an entire training facility that had everything Kira would need to test out his powers. The room has hologram technology, weights, obstacles, and robotic technology. There is also a computer screen that can track his strength and agility. The room also has tons of wooden dummies. Kira and Mia were both in shock, and he turned to look at Jack. He pointed at the training room in question, and Jack nodded.

Jack then said, "Yes. This is mine. Well, it was my dad's originally. He used it to train and study servicemen from the armed forces. He would have done the training himself, but he couldn't keep up."

Kira asked in disbelief, "And now you're letting me train here Jack?"

Jack nodded. "Of course! It'll help you become the hero I know you can be."

Kira looked at Mia and remembered how he had scared her when he couldn't control his anger with the lieutenant. He remembered how he had treated Kari and Chuck on the last day of school. He felt guilty and that he needed to make a change. He made up his mind. He would never scare her again. He would never treat his friends like that again either. The only way to make sure he was strong enough to defeat the creatures and conquer his own inner demons was to train and train hard.

"Thanks, Jack," He mumbled. "Let's see what I can do."

Jack said, "Let's do it!"

They bumped fists.

Jack activated the holograms from inside his office where he and Mia were safely out of the way. Kira began his transformation into Strike and got into a ready position. Jack set up seven holograms for Strike to fight.

Jack called to him, "Ready?"

He nodded, and the holograms converged on him.

One by one, he took the holograms down. He elbowed one from behind and sent him flying. He sent a flying kick at a hologram that had a knife (the knife wouldn't pierce Strike's skin). Two others charged toward him; and he blocked a punch, and with a push, he sent both flying. Another robotic hologram drew a samurai sword and got into a samurai pose. Strike pulled one of the swords from his back holster. He and the hologram charged at one another, swords drawn. There was a loud "clanking noise" as the swords clashed together. After a moment, the robot and the sword got slashed to pieces. One drone tried to use a rocket launcher and sent one toward Strike. He grabbed and crushed the rocket, causing a small explosion. Smoke covered the room, and the drone couldn't find Strike. Suddenly, he came out of the smoke and delivered an uppercut, sending the drone into the air and denting the ceiling. The last drone was way bigger than the others. It sent a punch at Strike, and he blocked it. The drone sent punch after punch at him that he continued to dodge.

When Strike got the chance, he sent a left hook at the drone's head, sending it flying. The impact caused a massive shockwave. The drone's body just collapsed. Strike put the sword back in its sheath, then clasped his hands, and bowed to the drones out of respect. Jack rushed up to Strike and began to ask him about his moves. Jack asked if he can analyze his sword and see what else it can do. Strike handed one over, and Jack went to work. Jack put it into the machine to the left of his desk and began to analyze it. Jack was astounded at the machine's discoveries. He grabbed the printout from the machine before it had even finished printing and ran down the stairs, two at a time, toward Strike and Mia.

"It's from another planet! It's from"—Jack panted and bent over to grab his knees—"another planet."

Strike and Mia looked at Jack in surprise and then looked at each other. Jack took a few breaths and uses a railing to steady himself.

"The metal is definitely not from this planet. I'm guessing it's from the same place as the creatures that murdered your parents."

Strike's anger flared. He let out a loud growl, and he clenched his fists.

Mia put her hand on Strike's shoulder and asked, "So what does this mean?"

Jack cleared his throat and excitedly said, "It means this sword is capable of more than any of us previously guessed! This means we've discovered a new metal never before discovered on Earth! It means that—"

Strike interrupted, "It means that we need to find out exactly what this sword can do."

Strike is positioned in the middle of the room. Jack and Mia are observing his vitals from Jack's office and through the use of probes attached to Strike's hands, chest, and body. The probes monitor his temperature, heart rate, and brain waves. Strike is holding both swords in front of him, and he's focusing his light energy on them. They began to glow with a bright light, and after a moment, the light was so bright that it was the only visible part of the swords. The temperature reader on his hands was registering temperatures higher and higher, close to the temperature that only the sun could withstand. However, his chest and body were registering a normal body temperature. The differences in temperature were beginning to disrupt the computer system, and the probes on Strike began to melt, catching fire before falling to the floor. The swords continued to glow, and the probes smoked and sizzled on the floor, causing the ceiling sprinklers to go off and drenching Strike in water. As the water drops touched Strike, they evaporated into steam. Jack and Mia were surprised by the turn of events and began shutting the computer equipment down.

Strike yelled, "What? Too much?"

Mia huffed, and Jack gave a smirk and said, "Just a bit."

When all three were toweling dry, Jack sat at his desk, running tests on Strike's hands. Mia explained that Strike can shoot laser beams out of his hands, and Jack was curious about how his body reacted that way.

He stated, "We need to find out what kind of energy it is and where it came from."

They scanned Strike's full body and Jack poured over the results. According to the results, the power comes from the cosmos, and the x-ray revealed that the powerful relic in Strike's chest is responsible for his power. Strike looked at his hands, sensing the life of others around him. He hadn't realized the true power of the Spirit Core. Jack thought the next test they should administer would be what happens when they put the weapon and energy together.

Strike grabbed his sword and stood in the samurai position in the center of the room. Jack activated the wrecking ball and sent it whirling toward him. As it came closer, Strike drew his second sword, and in slow motion, he began to fill his swords with light energy. With a flash, he slashed the wrecking ball and chain completely in half. The two halves of the wrecking balls slammed into each wall. Mia and Jack were in awe of his strength. Jack and Mia jumped around excitedly behind the two-way safety mirror. Strike began to pull the light energy back from his swords, and once they were normal again, he put them back into their sheath.

Turning, he said, "You know I can see you two, right?"

Causing Jack and Mia to spring apart in embarrassment.

*****

Mia, Jack, and Kira said good night to each other in the foyer of Jack's mansion. Kira trudged up the spiral staircase and threw himself on his borrowed bed. His body was so exhausted; he thought he would fall asleep on the car ride back to Jack's house. Now that he was actually in bed, his brain wouldn't shut off. He couldn't stop wondering what Kari and Chuck were doing and wishing things could be like they were a few months back. He wished his parents were still alive, and he didn't have to carry such a large, secret burden.

He tossed and turned. Even though the summer barely started, he wasn't looking forward to going back to school. He felt that his school years should be over now because he had much bigger things to worry about.

He heard his phone beep and chirp. He saw that it was Kari's number, and he sent it to voicemail with a painful pang. Chuck and Kari had each been calling him at least once a day, and his voicemail was slowly filling up. He couldn't bring himself to listen to the voicemails. He wanted to see them both so badly, but in his heart, he knew he would only put them in danger. He knew that the only way to keep them safe was to push them away because he couldn't protect them when he couldn't even protect himself. Eventually, he fell into a fitful sleep, plagued by nightmares of his parents dying with him being unable to move or do anything to stop it.

Chapter 9

Jack showed Strike and Mia the way to an abandoned air hanger for him to practice flying. Jack told the pair that he had made some modifications to the flight obstacles, such as six high-voltage hoops, remote-controlled turrets, holographic fire, and pillars. Strike flew through two hoops without getting electrocuted. While flying, he used his swords to deflect bullets back at the turrets, destroying each one. He weaved in and out of the pillars in a figure 8 formation, honing his flying skills. As he turned to fly toward the fire simulation to save the holographic innocent citizens, a pack of five drones took off from the ground. The drones looked like robotic harpies. He was caught by surprise and took a hit in his side from one of the harpies. He began to lose altitude and plummeted. At the last moment, he recovered and began to fly higher.

The drones began to chase after Strike and continued to try to swat him out of the air. He dodged every attack except for one, which caught him on the arm. He grunted in pain and realized that the talon actually pierced his skin. He sliced the offending drone in two and watched it fall and explode into small pieces on the ground.

He yelled to Jack, "Hey! I'm really impressed that you were able to duplicate my sword's metal so quickly, but I'm not ready to test my flying combat just yet!"

He flew around the nearest pillar and began to circle back toward the other end of the hanger with the remaining four drones in tow.

Jack's panicked voice came over the loudspeaker, "I appreciate your vote of confidence, buddy, but I can't take credit for this one! They aren't any of mine!"

Strike stopped midair and hovered for a moment. He yelled in confusion, "Wait…what?"

The drones came closer and closer to where he was hovering and gave Jack no time to respond. One drone flew at Strike, and he dropped out of its view. He reached up and ripped the drone apart. The other three drones stopped in midair a few feet away from him and began to pelt him with bullets from Gatling blasters.

He used his swords to deflect the bullets and called to Jack, "If they aren't yours, then whose are they?"

Jack shrugged and realizing Strike's attention was elsewhere, he replied over the loudspeaker, "I don't know where they come from or who sent them, but I can tell you one thing, their technology is OFF the CHARTS. They're definitely here for you and… I think they're… *transmitting*…"

Strike narrowed his eyes in anger and dropped suddenly from his place in the sky, causing the drones to stop shooting and try to follow him down.

He thought he knew where the drones may have come from and he responded angrily, "Transmitting what exactly?"

Jack ran to the computer and began typing quickly, responding to Strike, "Give me a minute and I can try to find out…"

Jack hacked into the drone's transmitter and quickly, his computer was flooded with a schematic map of Strike's body in motion and an analysis of his abilities. Jack tried for several moments in vain to locate where the signal was transmitting to, but he was not able to locate the source. He zoomed in on the live cam of the drone that was farthest from Strike. He was able to zoom in close enough on the back of the closest drone, and he discovered a logo. He quickly took a screenshot of it and continued to sift through the information he had discovered. Strike continued to lead the drones further away from Jack and dodged each of their blasters. He weaved in and out of drones and began evasive flying techniques he wasn't aware he had. He flew in loop de loops, up and over, under and up, again and again. Changing directions suddenly, he sucker punched the nearest drone, causing a technical malfunction, which sent it careening toward the ground.

Meanwhile, Jack typed furiously on his keyboard, spreading codes across both huge computer screens in front of him, trying to break into the drone's network. He cracked the encryption for the drone's network with a grunt of frustration, wiping sweat from his brow. Once the encryption was broken, thousands of images of Kira (and Kira as Strike) flooded the computer screens. Each picture showed Kira in different places, different outfits, with different people. Jack and Mia were both in hundreds of photos, meaning that these drones must have been able to access Jack's own personal network surveillance. Cursing under his breath as the pictures continued to flood in, Jack began typing again, trying to get to the source of what the drones were looking for and what they were transmitting. He jumped up suddenly as a video of Strike in the abandoned mall popped up on the leftmost computer screen. The video began to play, and Jack discovered that the video was edited to describe in detail Strike's fighting style and possible weaknesses.

Above, Strike continued to be chased by the two remaining drones. He was beginning to get tired of avoiding the blasts and was too slow to avoid one of them, which caught him in the back. With a grunt of pain, he sank a bit lower in the sky, beginning to panic slightly. He lost speed as he reached back to check the wound. Without warning, one of the drones caught his right leg with an electrical tendril which sent fifty thousand volts of electricity through his body. Strike dropped low in surprise, unable to prepare his body for the shock. With an angry flash, he grabbed his sword, which glowed brightly with energy, and slashed the tendril, causing it to release its grip on him. He went into supersonic speed and grabbed Mia and teleported her out of there. The remaining drones followed without delay. As the drones were chasing him, he came up with a plan. He led the drones toward the fake building. He asked her if she trusts him.

She nodded and said, "Yes…why?"

Strike sent energy coursing through his sword and sliced the building foundation in two. Immediately, the building began to crumble. While the outer part of the building started to crash down around them, he held his ground inside the building, waiting for the drones to come. When they came in fast, one from each side, he tele-ported himself and Mia out of the way, causing the drones to fly into each other. He took off toward Jack, and the building tipped toward the incapacitated drones and crushed them. He carefully dropped Mia into the grass with an "oof."

He asked, "Mia...are you all right?"

She grumbled, getting up slowly. "Am I all right? Sure, I'm fine. It's not every day that your brother brings a building down on top of you," she said, glaring at Strike but smiling playfully. She asked, stepping closer to the building to get a better look, "In all seriousness though, what were those things?"

When he gave no answer and fixed her with a grave expression, her gaze dropped, her eyes filling with unshed tears.

"It was them, wasn't it? The creatures that murdered our parents?"

He reached out and put his arm around her shoulders, nodding grimly, "I'm afraid so."

Strike and Mia made their way quickly back to Jack, who was still furiously typing on the computer.

Having long lost the connection to the drone's server, Jack began, "So I was able to hack into their system and retrieve some files. They caught on to my hack and were able to sever the connection before I could locate them... But I think I found out what they were doing. They were lo—"

Strike held up his right hand and interrupted Jack, saying, "I know what they were after, Jack. I need to find out where they're coming from."

Jack's shoulders slumped in frustration as he was proud of his discoveries; frowning in irritation, he turns back to the computers.

"Those were sent by the same monsters that killed our parents, Jack," Strike said, clenching his fist in anger.

Jack turned back toward Strike and Mia, his face full of mingled shock and pity.

Clenching his jaw tightly, Jack said, "We'll find them, Kira. I still have some ideas I haven't tried yet."

Strike nodded in silent agreement and turned to walk back toward the exit.

Mia, having been quietly observing the exchange, called to him in confusion, "Wait! Kira! Where are you going? Don't leave!"

He stopped and couldn't bring himself to face her. "I need a minute," he said, leaving no more room for argument and taking off into the air at full speed.

Jack asked Mia if she was okay. She stood facing the direction that Strike was a moment before.

Dropping her head low and taking a deep breath, she nodded slowly. "Yeah, I'll be okay."

She turned and walked back to where Jack sat looking at her. He smiled an awkward nervous smile.

He said, "I did find something useful. I found out what this group is called…"

At this, she looked up expectantly.

Jack continued, "They're called 'The Shadow Dragons.'"

She was surprised.

He gestured to the open hanger. "Should we go tell him?"

Mia shook her head. "No, let's keep it to ourselves for now."

He nodded in agreement and turned back to what he was working on. With a final glance at the exit, Mia rubbed her left arm with her right hand, knowing she and her brother would never be the same. She turned her attention to the work Jack was doing and sunk down into the seat next to him.

*****

Planet Dragza

But you see the dark side of one of Dragza's moons. There is green lava, a dark castle, spiked crystals, lots of Shadow Dragons training, drinking, eating, gambling. There is a throne room where Dark Strike is (he is the ruler of the Shadow Dragons). Gen. Oblivion, Slithor, and the lieutenant, who lost the battle to Strike, were all in the throne room together.

The lieutenant was delivering the message to Dark Strike about the boy who became Strike Dragon. He told him of Strike's power and how he killed all the soldiers that were with him. Dark Strike tightly gripped both armrests of his throne in anger. You could hear a cracking sound as they began to break. He let out an angry growl that caused the lieutenant to shake in fear. The lieutenant explained to him that the boy wanted him to deliver a message. He said he now goes by Strike and that he will be coming for you for killing his parents. Gen. Oblivion began to berate the lieutenant, asking him how he made it out alive.

The second in command, Slithor, yelled, "So you're telling us you basically failed your mission, is that right?" Wrapping his tail around the lieutenant's neck before calling him an idiot.

Dark Strike stood up and held up his hand, signaling to his second-in-command to back off the lieutenant.

"I've heard enough," Dark Strike said in anger.

Slithor then removed his tail from the lieutenant's neck. As the lieutenant was trying to catch his breath, he began to stutter, saying that Strike looks a lot like Leon Dragon.

Dark Strike said, "Well done, Lieutenant," as he walked out of the shadows of his throne room into the light.

The lieutenant said, "Wait...that's it?"

Dark Strike replied, "Of course, you should be rewarded for your hard work."

The lieutenant then began to breathe a sigh of relief, thinking of all the rewards he could receive from Dark Strike. The lieutenant began to get excited.

Then Dark Strike said, "You deserve a long rest, maybe a vacation?"

The lieutenant, feeling confused started to explain, "But I'm not tired," just as Dark Strike shot the lieutenant in the head with an energy blast from his finger.

As Dark Strike blew the smoke away from his finger, the lieutenant fell to the ground dead.

In walked Dr. Syclonus through the doors of the throne room.

Dark Strike said, "Ah, Dr. Syclonus. Do you have any good news for me unlike my lieutenant?" Dark Strike points at the dead lieutenant.

Dr. Syclonus answered, "I have news of the boy that you seek, Lord Dark Strike."

Dark Strike eases back into his throne and said, "Excellent. I'm all ears!"

He explains about the drones and shows Dark Strike the projections of the hologram of Strike. As the hologram continued playing, Dark Strike became more and more intrigued. Seeing Strike's abilities, he thought to himself that he reminded him of his father.

He stated, "I want us all to prepare to leave for Earth immediately."

*****

Back on Earth, Jack and Mia were still at the computer when Dr. Syclonus played the hologram for Dark Strike. Jack was able to hack into the drone's system. They were able to watch Dr. Syclonus showing Dark Strike the hologram of Strike. Both jumped up in surprise and started debating about the creature. Dr. Syclonus noticed that Jack hacked into the drone's system. He decided to overload the computer with info to destroy hackers. Jack's computer started heating up and it burned him. As he tried to stop it from ruining his computer, Mia began to scream. Strike heard her and rushed back, busted through the wall, and saved them with his super speed. Strike took them outside before the computer exploded. Safety measures take effect.

Strike flew them back to Jack's mansion under the cover of darkness. He began to change back into Kira. Jack was pacing around the living room, thinking about Dark Strike. Kira finished changing and grabbed a cup of tea. He was spacing out, feeling like he wasn't 100 percent himself. Mia got concerned and put her hand on his shoulder. He displayed a huge smile. Jack and Mia filled him in on the Shadow Dragons and Dark Strike. Jack shows Kira a video on his phone of Dark Strike. Kira got angry and crushed his teacup. When he noticed the cup, he was surprised. Mia changed the subject and both Kira and Jack decided that Strike was ready to use his powers in real combat.

Kira stood and Mia asked, "Are you sure Kira is ready because he is still struggling to control his temper?"

The two of them discussed passionately for a few minutes, arguing back and forth about it. Jack stopped them by explaining that there is a way to test whether Kira is ready.

Jack turned on the TV, and it revealed a bank robbery in progress. There were about ten robbers identified. The robbery is in progress at San Diego Trust and Savings Bank. They are holding forty people as hostages. The robbers said if their demands aren't met, they will kill them all. Jack and Mia were watching the TV, and Jack began to speak.

He said, "Kira, I think this would be the perfect time to—"

He turned to see that Kira had already vanished. He threw up his hands in frustration and said, "*Annnnd* he's gone."

At the bank, twenty policemen, five police cars, two SWAT teams, one fire engine, and two ambulances were blocking the intersection and had the entrance and exits covered. The police chief was using a megaphone to try to reason and negotiate with the robbers that were inside the bank. He was trying to persuade them to let the hostages go. Strike overhears him saying the robbers would release the hostages once safe transportation was provided. The robbers are threatening to kill the hostages, one every thirty minutes if they don't get them safe transportation.

When Strike heard this, it made him extremely angry, and his eyes began to glow; and he took off faster than the speed of light. Suddenly, everyone hears a sonic boom (similar to the sound jets make).

One of the officers located where the sound came from shouted, "Look up over there!"

Everyone looked and saw something made of light energy heading for the building. It was Strike. He broke through the window on one of the floors and went inside the building as quickly as possible.

The lead robber, upon hearing the weird noise further up in building, sent one of the robbers to go and check it out.

The robber was looking around trying to locate the source. He yelled, "What the…" Then there was a loud *THUMP*.

He tried to radio the first guy, but there was no response. He then sent two more robbers to find the first robber. The two other robbers rushed upstairs to see what was going on. They rushed in the room and found the first robber upside down, halfway through the floor. Only his legs were visible, and his AK-47 was torn to pieces all over the floor. They cautiously looked around the room then looked at each other in fear. The room suddenly went really dark, and the robbers heard a *WOOSH* sound, causing them to shoot into the darkness.

The angry voice of the lead robber came over the radio, asking, "What the hell's going on up there?"

One of the robbers responded, "Something or *someone* is up here! We are one man down already."

The lead robber asked angrily, "What do you mean?"

The other robber replied, "Something happened to Frank!"

The two robbers backed out of the room quickly.

They told the lead robber over the radio, "Frank got smashed into the floor! All we could see was his legs sticking out, and he wasn't moving. Whoever did this to him is still in the building!"

The lead robber frantically replied, "Well, where is he? Where did he go, Eddie?"

Eddie began talking into the radio, "I don't know! He may have gone—"

Then the radio let off a loud squeal as if the frequency had been scrambled. The two robbers heard a LOUD growl from behind them. They both readied themselves, turning quickly, and shooting at Strike until their guns ran out of bullets. All the bullets fell to the ground in front of Strike's feet, not harming him at all. Their eyes got extremely big at this. Eddie told the other robber to run as he began to fumble to put another round of bullets in his gun. Strike snatched his gun with great speed and crushed it like a toy, letting it drop to the ground. Eddie tried to draw his pistol quickly, and Strike sliced the gun in half with one sword while slicing his disguise with the other. Strike pointed at the radio and Eddie blinked in terror. Eddie unclasped the radio and handed it to him in a daze. Strike held out his hand at a ninety-degree angle, like a handshake, and then hit him through the door. The other robber had run back downstairs.

He was frantic and was telling the lead robber, "There is a creature up there!"

The lead robber called over the radio, asking, "Eddie! What is going on? Is the creature dead?"

Strike spoke over the radio, "Sorry, Eddie can't come to the phone right now. Please try again later."

The lead robber yelled over the radio, "Who the HELL are you?"

Strike responded, "Just a concerned citizen…THAT'S GOING TO TAKE YOU DOWN!"

The lead robber responds, "You're going to regret what you've done to my men…"

Strike answers, "You know what's regrettable? Your attitude and what you're threatening to do to those people."

The lead robber replied, "If you want me, come get me. We'll be ready."

Strike said, "Oh, don't worry. I'll be there soon."

Strike dropped the radio and stomped on it, breaking it into a thousand pieces. He walked toward the door, and Eddie began to stir, shaking his head a little.

Strike said, "Do me a favor, Eddie…don't get up."

Eddie gave a wobbly thumbs-up and stayed on the ground.

The robber who ran frantically back downstairs grabbed two more guys and started heading back up the stairs. When they got to the second floor, they heard the elevator coming down for the upper floors. The three robbers pushed the elevator button and waited for it to come to them. They all readied their weapons as the elevator stopped on their floor. The door slid open. One of the robbers shot accidentally and the other two followed. One of them held up his hand when he noticed there was no one in the elevator. One gestured for the other to check things out. He went in and looked around. All he saw were bullet holes and sparks.

He looked at the others in confusion and said, "He's not in here."

The one in the elevator stopped and said, "Wait! Do you hear that?"

They shook their heads and one said, "Hear what?"

Just then, Strike's arm busted through the top of the elevator car and pulled the robber up on top of it and knocked him out. Strike dropped down through the hole, and the other two robbers started shooting at him. The bullets had no effect, and many ricocheted off. He walked toward one of the robbers and smacked his gun away and lifted him in the air and tossed him at a nearby window. It broke, and the robber was hanging out of it, his uniform caught on a glass pane. He began slipping and was about to fall when Strike picked him up and brought him back inside then headbutted him into unconsciousness. The final robber pulled out his pistol and aimed at Strike's eye, shooting at point-blank range. When the bullet touched Strike's eye, his eyes flashed bright white light, and the bullet melted.

The robber saw the bullet melt and Strike looked at him and said, "Nice try."

The robber tried to put up his gun again, but Strike was too fast for him. Strike pinned him to the wall and asked him where his boss was. The robber was scared and was sputtering random things. Strike got frustrated and used his claws to slash the wall next to his head.

Strike said, "I don't have time for this. Where is he?"

The robber finally yells, "Okay! Okay! I'll tell you! He's on the bottom floor!"

Strike looked at him suspiciously and said, "You better be telling the truth!"

The robber pleaded, "I am! I swear!"

Strike used his senses to find out if the robber was telling the truth, and he found that he was.

Strike let him go from the wall and growled, "Thank you for telling the truth. Before I go, please accept my apology."

The robber stood there confused and asked, "Um… For what? For what you did to my friends or…"

Strike shook his head and said, No. For this." Strike sucker punched him and knocked him out.

Strike used his speed to run down the stairs in a flash. He arrived on the bottom floor where the lead robber and the other four robbers were waiting with the hostages. They were all looking around to find out where Strike would come out. The lead robber had the others guarding hostages and areas while he was trying to get into the safe. The bank worker refused to help. The lead robber was frustrated and was yelling at her. The security guard told him to stop, and the lead robber shot him in the leg, causing him to fall to the ground bleeding. The bank worker was extremely scared, and the lead robber yelled at her for the code again. She nodded that she'd help him get into the safe. She was shaking and crying. She kept putting in the wrong code, and he was getting angrier, telling her to hurry up.

He said, "You better hurry or I'll—"

Strike busted through the door to the stairway, blasting the door off its hinges, smacking into one of the robber's face, knocking him out.

Strike said, "Or you'll what?"

The lead robber glared at him and shouted to his comrades, "KILL HIM."

The hostages fell flat on the ground, and the robbers started shooting at him.

Strike rolled his eyes and muttered, "Here we go again."

The bullets still had no effect on him, and he came up close to one of the robbers, punching him in the chest so hard, he flew into a large clock, shattering it. Strike turned and shot another robber with a shockwave burst, making him fly into the safe. Another robber attempted to use a heavy machine gun, and Strike realized that if the robber shot at him, the bullets may hit the hostages behind him. Strike pulled out his swords and deflected the bullets back at the robber. He came close to the robber and sliced the gun into pieces. He put his swords back into his sheath, and the gun fell apart, making the robber gasp. Strike held up his finger at the robber and shook it at him.

The robber wet his pants in fear and ran outside to the policemen saying, "I surrender, take me away!"

This left only the lead robber. Strike looked from the door to the lead robber and pulled out his sword. The lead robber grabbed one of the hostages by her shoulder and held a gun to her head.

"I swear, if you move, I'll put a bullet in her brain!"

Strike was growling at him and glaring. Strike let go of his sword and let it slide into his sheath. He sighed and let his anger out.

He said, "Okay. What do you want?"

The lead robber smiled an ugly smile and said, "All I want is to get out of here with a car and my money with you not doing anything to stop me. Got it?"

Strike responded, "All right, but you leave all the hostages unharmed."

The lead robber forced the bank worker to open the safe and had her grab the money and hand it to him.

He walked the hostage past Strike while holding the money, and said, "Nice doing business with you…"

While the lead robber was distracted, the worker found his weak spot and elbowed him as hard as she could. He let go of her with a howl of pain. He was about to shoot her when Strike came close and gave him an uppercut to the stomach, a left hook to the face, twisted his arm, and crushed his hand, causing him to drop the gun. Strike sent him flying through the front glass door with a kick. The lead robber became a hood ornament for a police cruiser, landing right on top of it outside. Strike then followed.

The surrounding police didn't know what to do and were uncertain. They aimed their guns at Strike, but the commissioner stopped anyone from shooting. The lead robber sputtered up blood and slipped down to the ground. He tried to grab his pistol from its hidden holster but found that it was lying on the ground a few inches away. He reached for it as Strike came over. Strike stomped on the pistol, crushing it into pieces. The lead robber looked up at Strike as he glared down at him. Strike picked him up by his neck and growled in his face. The lead robber began to chuckle, sending blood spitting out.

He said, "Go ahead. Do it. Kill me."

Strike had his claws out and was contemplating killing him. Strike looked around and caught eyes with the commissioner.

The commissioner gave him a stern look and yelled, "Don't do it!"

Strike let out a sigh and retracted his claws.

"No, you're right, commissioner." He then looked the robber in the eyes and grumbled, "That would be the easy way out! You don't deserve it."

Strike let him fall to the ground.

Chapter 10

The commissioner sent in several of his officers to cuff the lead robber. He nodded to Strike and said thank you. Strike told the commissioner that the robbers wounded one of the security guards, and he was still inside. He told him he may want to call over the EMTs. Strike told the commissioner that he took care of the rest of the robbers, and the hostages are free to leave. The commissioner responded okay and told the rest of his unit to move in. Strike moved in a flash and went back to the security guard lying on the ground to wait for medical attention and assure the EMTs would arrive safely. He was telling the security guard he was going to be okay.

The guard was crying and in a lot of agony. The guard was saying he couldn't die because he had family. Out of compassion, Strike reached out and put pressure on the man's wound. Strike's hand and chest began to glow to his surprise. The guard's wound began to heal, and Strike gasped in amazement. He let go of the guard and looked at his hand, which continued to glow. He looked down at the guard, who was looking at his leg in amazement.

The guard said, "I can't feel the pain anymore! The pain is gone!"

The officers and medical personnel came in and began taking the hostages outside. The guard asked shyly if Strike could help him up, and he did. Strike supported the guard's weight until the man found his feet. The pair walked out through the chaos, watching the robbers being led away in handcuffs and put into the back of the SWAT vehicle. EMTs rushed up to Strike and the security guard. They ushered the guard over to the ambulance.

Before they could close the doors, the security guard called to Strike and said, "Thank you!"

Strike nodded and humbly responded, "You're welcome."

The ambulance dashed in the direction of the hospital. Strike turned and noticed that many of the policemen were aiming their weapons at him again. All at once, the hostages erupted in outrage, telling the police that Strike was a hero, and he had saved all their lives. The commissioner reemerged from the bank and called for his men to lower their weapons. He placed his hand on the barrel of the last gun and pushed it down.

The commissioner said, "He is not our enemy. I'm not sure what he is, but I know that he's a hero today."

Strike nodded and thanked him. All the hostages and others present started applauding Strike for saving their lives.

As Strike was getting ready to leave, the commissioner asked, "Who are you?"

Strike turned and looked at him. He proudly responded, "My name is Strike Dragon, and I am a friend."

Strike then took off into the air, going to Mach-24, making a loud sonic boom.

Strike's face was shown on every news station. The reporters were describing what he did in detail and ended with Strike flying off. Jack and Mia were watching with excitement and jumped up to give each other a congratulatory hug. Once the hug was over, Jack leaned in and kissed her. After a moment, they pulled away from each other embarrassed.

Jack looked at her and suggested, "Why don't we keep this between us…"

As Mia smirked, his face became a grimace, stating, "He's behind me, isn't he?"

She nodded.

Jack turned around as Strike looked up from a magazine he was flipping through.

Strike grinned and said, "Yep. Don't mind me… Do you want me to finish reading this magazine before or after I laugh at you two?"

Jack blushed, and Mia coughed, trying to change the subject.

Moving away from Jack to sit next to Strike, she excitedly said, "So tell us everything! How did it go?"

Strike smiled his first genuine smile since his parents died. "I don't know how to describe it, Mia. It felt...right."

Strike couldn't put into words how he felt helping those hostages. It was like everything he had experienced, all the trauma and all the worry (about his friends, about Mia, about school, about everything), just fell away, and he was finally able to just be 100 percent who he was meant to be.

Strike explained everything that happened at the bank, sparing no details. He ended with the final showdown between him and the lead robber, telling the pair that he had saved the woman from being shot right on time. After Strike finished his story, Jack decided he wanted to see everything in real time. He hacked into the bank's security cameras and played the entire video. Mia was horrified about what happened to some of the robbers until Strike explained that all of them were still alive, and he made sure they still had pulses.

After they saw Strike heal the guard, he remembered to tell them about the most important part...his healing powers. The news was still playing in the background. One of the reporters was interviewing the police commissioner. The reporter was asking what they were going to do about this menace and whether the police commissioner had doubts about Strike.

The police commissioner's face hardened, and he cut the interview short, saying, "Look. All I know is that this Strike Dragon is the reason every single person in that bank made it out alive. If you have any doubts about this guy, take it from me, he was a real hero today! That's all I have to say at this time."

He got in his vehicle, slamming the door, narrowly missing the reporter's microphone.

The reporter said, "That's a wrap for now. We will have more information later."

Jack turned from the TV and said, "Okay, Strike looks like you have a fan..."

Strike nodded, saying, "It's more than that. He has a good heart. He can tell who is good and who is evil. I'm glad to have him as an ally."

Jack turned and said, "What's that supposed to mean?"

Strike's face was deep in thought, and Jack understood what he was talking about.

Jack said, "You're going to reveal yourself to him, aren't you?"

Strike nodded slowly and responded, "Maybe."

Jack stood up from where he was sitting and was about to tell him what a crazy idea that was when Strike said, "I know, I know… I'm not talking about showing him right now. It may take more time to earn his trust…"

Mia interrupted, standing up to face Strike. "You're talking about showing him who and what you really are, Kira. You're my brother. I want you to be safe. This isn't safe."

He began to argue and thought better of it. "She's right… You're right, Mia… I'll try my best not to reveal myself to anyone. I'll only consider the police commissioner as my ally. Nothing more."

Relieved, she closed the distance between them and wrapped herself around Strike in a hug.

After they finished their hug, Jack asked, "So what happens now?"

Strike looked from Jack to Mia and back to Jack. "Now, we wait."

Mia looked confused and was about to ask what they were waiting for when Strike began again, "We wait for more of these creatures to come to us…and in the meantime, I will build up my strength…"

Jack finally asked, "What does that mean exactly?"

A news flash came over the television describing a high-speed chase off the 8 Freeway in San Diego.

Strike smiled at Jack and said, "You'll soon find out." He then took off into the air in a flash.

High-speed chase scene: camera followed the car on 8 Freeway as it exited by Qualcomm, car is moving fast toward a group of senior citizens and was about the hit them. Strike flew in and picked up the car, flying it over to the police station and ripping off the tires so the criminal couldn't escape.

The thief was trying to rob a liquor store, waving a gun all over, and began to try to shoot innocent people. Strike cut the thief's gun in two using the pieces to tie up the crook.

Assault: a woman walked down a dark alley in downtown San Diego. Three men followed her and began to jeer at her, one pushed her down and the other two grabbed each of her arms. Strike appeared and beat the men up, throwing one into a dumpster. Strike flew the girl to the police station, and he disappeared.

Out-of-control trolley: a trolley is malfunctioning at rush hour, and the conductor wasn't able to control the train. The trolley was about to crash into the docks when Strike stopped the trolley from crashing with his hands and pushed the brakes with his feet. Strike saluted the people and took off into the air.

Airplane crash: a small airplane was careening toward Palomar Mountain. Strike came up and stopped the plane with his mind/force magic. Strike flew the plane back to the airport.

The picture began to fade out, and Strike is featured on every newspaper's headlines on the front cover. Strike saved a cruise ship from sinking, saved astronauts from an exploding vessel, Strike beat up a giant mutant. (STRIKE DOESN'T HAVE ANY TIME TO HIMSELF. NO TIME TO CHECK HIS PHONE, TO CALL CHUCK OR KARI, OR TO WORRY ABOUT GOING BACK TO SCHOOL. MONTAGE SHOWS THAT HE BARELY HAS TIME FOR SLEEP.)

The mayor of Escondido and hundreds of people from surrounding cities gathered at City Hall to present Strike with an award for helping the citizens. The mayor described how much Strike has done and how many lives he has saved.

He pointed to the sky and said, "This is for you, Strike Dragon!"

Strike flew down and landed at the bottom of the steps. He walked up to the mayor and shook his hand, saying thank you. He turned toward the commissioner, who smiled and placed a gold medal over his head. The audience cheered. The mayor described in detail why Strike deserves more than just a medal. He gestured for Strike to speak.

Strike said nervously, "I never wanted to be famous, and I didn't prepare a speech but...wherever there is someone in trouble, I'll be here to fight for them. To fight for their freedom. And to fight for justice. For everyone. Most importantly, I'll fight for peace."

The audience clapped and cheered for him. After he was done talking, he bowed to the commissioner and mayor. Strike then flew off.

The mayor turned to speak to the audience. He said, "So there it is, folks. All criminals, beware of San Diego's Strike DRAGON!"

Strike came back to Jack's house and called Mia and Jack's names, but there was no answer. After a few moments of getting worried, he thought he knew where they would be. He took off and flew to the training area where Mia was training.

Mia, although not much changed in appearance, was more muscular than in the last scene. She was dressed in a special battle armor that Jack had prepared for her. She was using specialized weaponry and had already taken down about four holographic drones. Jack was analyzing her movements and observing her progress. He lost focus on the computer as one of the drone heads came flying at him and narrowly missed slamming into his shoulder. He turned and looked at the head and looked at Mia then he looked back at the head and then back to Mia.

He exclaimed, "Whoa! That almost hit me!"

Mia giggled and said jokingly, "Oops. Sorry, I didn't mean for that to happen. We're going to have to teach you how to catch, Jack." She smiled and took a rag to wipe at the sweat on her forehead. She walked over to Jack and said, "So how'd I do?"

He glanced back at the computer screen, chuckling, and said, "Actually, you did really well! Much better than when you started! You're almost a real fighter now!"

Mia scoffed and playfully slapped him on the shoulder. "Hey! I am already a real fighter! Strike has taught me well!"

She cartwheeled back into the arena and began to fight with the remaining two drones. She drove her elbow into the chest of the drone on the left and did a spin kick, catching the head of the drone on the right, incapacitating both of them. She looked around for any remaining drones, and hearing footsteps behind her, she whirled around to punch the drone square in the jaw, realizing too late that it wasn't a drone. Strike caught her fist mere centimeters from his face and laughed.

"Not bad, I almost didn't catch your punch this time."

Dropping her fist, she excitedly said, "You're back!" She pulled him in to a hug. Apologizing, she said, "I'm sorry! I wasn't expecting you back so soon! School doesn't even start until tomorrow! I thought you were a drone!"

Strike chuckled and replied, "It's okay, Mia. Accidents happen. At least I didn't catch you by surprise again!"

Her smile soured, and she said, "That wasn't fair! You flew in last time!"

Jack broke in and asked, "How did it go at City Hall?"

Strike walked over and took a seat on the couch that was there for spectating training sessions. "It went well. I got a medal..."

At Mia's excited expression, Strike shifted uncomfortably. "I never really cared about being famous... I just wanted to help people. And now, I can only help people when I'm not busy with school..." he said, rolling his eyes with a grimace at the prospect of going back to school.

Jack came over and sat next to him. "At least now you have the whole country's respect, and you have me to help you with school now."

Strike nodded in agreement and said, "Yeah, that's true."

His thoughts rested on the idea of going back to school, and a part of him knew why he was feeling so uncomfortable. He had been avoiding Chuck and Kari all summer long. His eyebrows furrowed in thought, and he got up, making his way toward the training center's exit.

He began, "If you guys need me, I'll be in the meditation room."

He left the room and Jack asked, "Why on Earth would he want to meditate right now? He just got a medal! It's time to celebrate!"

Mia looked at the place where Strike was a moment ago, sighing, and in sad understanding, she said, "I know why. He wants to reconnect with the Spirit Core and talk to the one who guides him."

Strike sat down and turned down the lights to a dull glow. Breathing deeply for a few moments, he began to meditate, bringing himself inside his subconscious mind. The Spirit Core began to glow brighter and brighter. His mind was calling out to Leon, and the first few times, there was no reply. Finally, Leon spoke from behind him, letting him know he was there.

Strike's heart was heavy as the weight of the guilt from avoiding his friends crushed him. Leon perceived that Strike was feeling off and decided to speak to him about it.

Leon said, "Strike, guilt cannot change the past and worrying won't change the future. If there are actions weighing on you, you must take steps to bring the universe back into balance."

Strike was surprised that Leon could see how upset he was. He asked, "But what if I've done something unforgivable? What if there's no way to make things right?"

Leon smiled knowingly and said, "There is always a way, my son. There's always a way."

Strike took a moment to think and took comfort in Leon's words, resolving to make things right with Chuck and Kari no matter what.

Leon patiently waited until Strike was done and then asked for updates on his powers. Strike began to tell Leon about the improvements he made with his powers and techniques. He advised Leon that there had still been no sign of the Shadow Dragons and that he had saved many people's lives thus far. Leon said he was happy about the progress he has made and that he is getting closer to being as powerful as he was. Strike asked if there was any way to get more powerful.

Leon replied, "Of course, but you must ascend to Super Dragon."

Strike was confused and asked for Leon to explain.

Leon explained, "Being a Super Dragon is an ancient power and only the most powerful can achieve it. In fact..." He stopped midsentence.

Strike asked, "What's wrong?"

Leon began again, "I sense a great evil coming near this planet. It must be him."

Strike said, "Him?"

Leon replied, "There's no time to explain. You and your friends need to be prepared. You need to be ready. Be ready for the greatest battle between good and evil you have yet faced."

Strike muttered, "What? What are you talking about? What's going on?"

Leon explained, "You must get ready, and when the time comes, you must ascend to Super Dragon. The fate of the Multiverse depends on you. Dark Strike is coming!"

Strike's face hardened, and his fists tightened in rage. Strike hissed, "Dark Strike. Where is he…"

Leon continued, "He's on his way. But listen… You aren't ready to fight Dark Strike. Not yet."

Strike started to protest. "But, Leon! He's the one who killed my parents! I can do—"

Leon interrupted, "No. You aren't ready. You need more time to prepare. When the time comes, you must be ready to fight an army."

Strike squinted in confusion. "An army? What army?"

Leon stated, "The army of the Shadow Dragons are coming. They will only attack when he gives the order. Now go. Go and be careful. If you die, all hope is lost forever, and both our worlds will fall into darkness."

Leon began to fade and Strike was calling to him, "Wait! Leon! How? How do I defeat him? How do I defeat Dark Strike?"

Strike came back into his own body, and the Spirit Core stopped glowing.

Strike came back into the training room where Jack and Mia were arguing about whether Strike needs help or whether he works better alone. Seeing him caused the argument to cease. Jack thinks he doesn't need help and Mia does.

Strike cuts them off, saying, "It would be better for all of us to work together."

Jack and Mia noticed that Strike looks a little off.

Mia, being concerned, asked, "Are you sure you're my brother?"

Strike told them about the warning he received from Leon.

*****

The park ranger was patrolling Yosemite, and everything was fine until he saw five meteors fall from the sky, each a different color with one being demonic red. He called over the radio and could only hear static. He rushed over to the crash site to investigate. He found five craters with the one in the middle being the largest. He began poking around the craters and noticed one of them move. A robotic hand poked out, which freaked him out, and he hid behind a boulder. The robotic arm began to climb out, revealing a robotic dragon. It was a demonic-looking creature who emerged from one of the craters with the eyes of a hawk. The robot began to check its circuitry. Someone did a kick move and propelled themselves out of one of the craters. The other two came out simultaneously; one slithered out. All the creatures bowed and waited for Dark Strike. Everything shook, and the middle crater rock burst open, showing Dark Strike's aura. The dust cleared and revealed Dark Strike with his fist in the air. He flew from the rubble and over to his soldiers (park ranger still cowering in fear).

Dr. Syclonus stood and said, "Lord Dark Strike, we have arrived at our destination. The planet Earth."

Dark Strike responded, "So this is Earth…" Looking around in disgust, he continued, "Interesting… Too bad it's overrun with…primates." He turned to Dr. Syclonus and said, "Tell me, Dr. Syclonus. Are we close to the boy?"

The park ranger began to creep away.

Dr. Syclonus pulled up the hologram and said, "The boy is here in San Diego, and we are right here."

Oblivion grumbled, "Great. We aren't even in the right place. Some scientist you are!"

Dr. Syclonus hissed.

Slithor came up between the two to stop them from fighting and said, "Enough. Remember your mission. We're here to fight a war. Not each other."

Sanus began to laugh maniacally and asked, "So, Lord Dark Strike, what should we do now?"

Dark Strike looked around and said, "Why don't we ask that pathetic human hiding behind that boulder?"

The park ranger realized that he had been caught and tried to get away as fast as he could, dropping on the ground, trying in vain to crawl away. Oblivion jumped and landed with a crack on top of the boulder above the ranger's head.

After the ranger looked up at Oblivion, he snarled, "Hello there."

Picking the ranger up by the collar, he carried him with little effort to the center of the circle, throwing him at Dark Strike's feet while the rest of the group surrounded him. He used his foot to pin the ranger down and pulled his hat and hair so that the ranger had to look up at Dark Strike.

Oblivion said, "Our master has some questions for you, and it's important that you be polite." Oblivion tugged the ranger's head up, further causing the ranger to grunt in pain. "If you aren't polite," Oblivion continued, picking up a large skull-size rock, "then I have a gift for you!" Oblivion crushed the rock into dust, saying, "You get what I mean?"

The ranger nodded the best he was able to, and he was terrified.

Dark Strike walked over to the ranger menacingly.

Leaning down and balancing on one knee, Dark Strike asked in a powerful voice, "Where is the Silver Dragon?"

The ranger's face clouded in confusion, and he stammered, "Wh-Who? I don't know any Silver Dragon!"

Dark Strike rolled his eyes in annoyance, and Oblivion smacked the ranger upside the head.

Slithor yelled, "Lord Dark Strike! Maybe this boy does not go by Silver Dragon on this planet! I think I remember reading that he went by another name…"

Dark Strike grimaced and leaned in close to the ranger again. "Very well. Where is the Dragon you call Strike?"

The ranger panicked and said nervously, "You mean that flying freak that keeps getting on the news? He's down in Southern California. Near San Diego… Es-Escondido, I think."

At the mention of the word freak, Dark Strike's eyes narrowed and glowed red, growling as his bottom lip twitched. The rest of the group hissed and growled at the word freak as well. Oblivion tightened his grip on the ranger's hair and used his other hand to grab the ranger's throat.

He hissed, "So we're all freaks, huh?"

Oblivion brought his longest/sharpest claw up to the ranger's eye.

As Oblivion was about the shove his nail into the ranger's eyeball, Dark Strike waived his hand and said, "Enough. I've grown weary of this world and its drama already. We must get to the boy."

Oblivion dropped hold of the ranger instantly, causing him to crumple in a heap in the dirt.

Oblivion dropped to a knee in front of Dark Strike and said, "As you wish, Lord Dark Strike."

Dark Strike made his way past Oblivion and said, "Thanks for your *cooperation*," to the ranger who was struggling to get up. As Dark Strike rose off the ground, he began, "Shadow Dragons, let's head out."

The rest of the group simultaneously responded, "Yes, Lord Dark Strike."

The troops began to take off one by one until only Dark Strike and the ranger remained.

Dark Strike turned to the ranger and told him, "Don't worry, you will be rewarded for your *politeness* and *hospitality*."

Dark Strike took off into the sky, and the ranger thought the exchange was really strange. Realizing he was finally alone, the ranger took off back toward his vehicle, hoping to alert other park rangers before it was too late.

Slithor flew alongside Dark Strike and suggested, "You know, he could tell everyone about us..."

Dark Strike nodded and replied, "Indeed, he could."

Slithor responded, "Then why didn't you kill him when you had the chance? This could be dangerous to our mission."

Dark Strike insisted, "Don't worry. He is not going to tell a soul."

Slithor asked again, even more confused, "How do you know?"

Dark Strike stopped and hovered in the air. He turned around and looked back to where the ranger was.

"Because there won't be anyone left to tell."

Dark Strike began to create an orb between his two hands that glowed bright red like the rising sun with black static around it. He threw the orb at the very spot where the ranger's vehicle stood, engulfing the entirety of Yosemite Park in red light. The ranger looked up from his vehicle and noticed the orb, changing his mood from confusion to fear, and screaming in terror as the orb came closer. As it hit the vehicle killing the park ranger and destroying the crater site, everything in that area was disintegrated. Nothing was left but a large red smear of nothingness.

After the rest of the Shadow Dragons saw that Dark Strike destroyed the area, they laughed.

Slithor, surprised by the destruction, turned to Dark Strike and said, "I thought you were going to spare his life…"

Dark Strike returned, "A quick death is the only reward he earned with his politeness and hospitality. This world has been overdue for extermination."

Slowly, a smile crept over Slithor's features, and Dark Strike mirrored that smile with his own, which positively oozed malice.

"Now then, let's go find this Strike Dragon."

All the Shadow Dragons powered up and took off at the speed of light in the direction of San Diego.

Dark Strike was the last to power up, looking back down at the red smear, he muttered, "We're coming for you, boy." He then took off and followed the rest of the Shadow Dragons.

Chapter 11

The Dragon Knights are called home to help defend Dragza from a Shadow Dragon attack (diversion for Shadow Dragons to find the Spirit Core). They leave because they don't know that the Shadow Dragons are there. They go fight off the attack.

After the battle is over, they meet together and discuss why on Earth the Shadow Dragons would send troops to fight a battle they can't win. That's when they find out about Kira's parents being killed. Rose is FURIOUS, and Wingsavior gives them permission to travel back to Earth to see what can be done; they still don't have permission to interfere.

After hearing of the parents' death, the Dragon Knights know that Strike needs to prove himself worthy of being a Dragon Knight. Wingsavior has ordered them not to interfere, only watch and wait for the signal. Strike needs to learn what he is capable of and what it means to be human before he learns what it means to be a Dragzarian.

*****

There's a football game at Qualcomm Stadium on September 13, 2015. Jack got five tickets, one for Chuck, Kari, Kira, Mia, and himself. Everyone was enjoying the football game. During halftime, everyone heard a loud noise, like a jet hovering over the stadium. Everyone started murmuring and wondering what was happening.

The security guards looked at each other and said, "What the? That's not part of the show…"

The Shadow Dragons landed on the field.

The announcer said, "What is going on here? Who has just landed on the field?"

The Shadow Dragons exited the playing field, and the spectators applauded because they thought it was part of the show until the Shadow Dragons started killing people that were on the field, causing panic. Everyone was pushing and scrambling to get out of the stadium. One security guard grabbed Slithor by the arm. Slithor then punched him in the face, causing him to fly across the field. Another security guard tried to tase Dark Strike, and Dark Strike twisted his neck and broke it with a loud crack.

Kira stood up in alarm and looked at Mia and Jack and acknowledged, "I must go!"

He then ran from his friends, so no one would see him with them as he dashed to go transform in private. He knew he needed to transform to protect everyone in the stadium.

Slithor yelled for the entire stadium to be quiet and announced, "Come out, come out wherever you are, Dragon Knight scum! If you don't, people will continue *DYINGGGGG*."

Dark Strike looked around the stadium and didn't see Strike anywhere. He silently turned to face the remaining Shadow Dragons and then looked back at the remaining audience.

Sanus asked, "What are your orders, boss?"

Dark Strike then quietly ordered, "Kill them *all*."

The Shadow Dragons darted past Dark Strike, charging at the closest audience members who were desperately trying to escape.

Strike suddenly appeared on the playing field. He began to take the Shadow Dragons down one by one, starting with the first one that charged the audience. Sanus was the first to charge at the audience like a psychopath. He was reaching to get a claw out to slash someone trying to get away that was in the front row. Strike used his superspeed to sucker punch him in the jaw. This caused Sanus to soar back across the field, out cold. He narrowly missed smacking into Dark Strike (Dark Strike stepped to the side, rolling his eyes in displeasure). Strike slowly sank from his spot hovering in the air. He landed softly on the railing that separates the field from the seats and stood with his arms crossed over his chest. The rest of the Shadow Dragons stopped dead in their tracks, allowing the audience mem bers to run away to safety. They turned and stared in disbelief at Strike. Their disbelief turned quickly to anger.

Dark Strike smirked evilly at Strike and growled, "Somehow I knew that would get your attention." He added, "I have to say, I thought you would have come sooner. That way, we wouldn't have had to squish so many." Dark Strike kicked the body of the security guard he killed, sending it skidding to Strike's feet. "Bugs." He finished with a nasty chuckle at Strike.

Strike sent a ball of light energy from his finger at Dark Strike, who laughed maliciously, stepping to one side to avoid getting hit, narrowly missing getting the bolt in his face. The other Shadow Dragons roared in anger and started toward Strike. Dark Strike held up his pointer finger to stop their advance for the moment.

"Ah, boys, you have so much to learn. Is that all you—"

Dark Strike's words cut off as blood started sliding down his cheek, where the energy blast managed to cut his mask. He brought a finger up to dab at the cut. Pulling his finger away from his cheek, he found it covered in blood.

He pulled his dark, cold eyes back up to look at Strike and said, "Fascinating!"

He brought his attention back to the other Shadow Dragons, bringing his pointer finger up to point at Strike.

"Continue," Dark Strike said, releasing his Shadow Dragons on Strike.

All at once, Slithor, Dr. Syclonus, and Gen. Oblivion charged at Strike, hooting and hollering in a fevered glee.

Dr. Syclonus stayed back to analyze Strike's fighting style on his own. Choosing to stay out of the fight for the moment and realizing that Strike's abilities had grown, he wanted to get a better idea and understanding of Strike's new fighting style. Gen. Oblivion popped out blades from his wrists and tried attacking Strike with them. Strike dodged every blow, following up the misses with a blow of his own, punching and kicking at Gen. Oblivion. As he was dodging Oblivion's attack, Slithor tried to attack him from behind, wrapping his body around Strike's feet and torso like a constrictor snake.

Taking advantage of Strike's distraction, Oblivion jumped in the air and attempted an aerial attack that would have incapacitated Strike.

Stomping on Slithor's tail and using his free hand to tighten around the middle of his body, Strike was able to break free of his grip for the moment. He took a step back, drawing both of his blades and leaping up to meet Oblivion, their blades clashing in the air between them, both hovering in the air above Slithor's body. Oblivion landed with a "*boom*" on top of Slithor's head, causing a sickening crunch and Slithor's body to go completely limp.

Oblivion looked down in disgust and shrugged, saying, "That's what happens if you don't get out of the way."

Slithor came to and laughed as he was choking and wheezing. Oblivion glared in annoyance that Slithor was still alive.

"What's so funny?"

Slithor raised his arm painstakingly and pointed at Oblivion's left arm. Oblivion looked down and noticed that there was no longer an arm there. There were only wires with electricity and sparks flying. His face scrunched up in confusion, and Dr. Syclonus was laughing silently at what failures the other two were. Strike stood silently, staring at Oblivion. Oblivion's face hardened, and he walked to pick up his arm.

He turned and pointed the sword at Strike, yelling, "You'll pay for what you did to my arm!"

He activated his thrusters, throwing his arm next to Slithor's body, and charged at Strike. Strike dodged and then elbowed him through the railing to land with a crunch on the first row of seats. The impact caused an overload in his circuits, and the damage caused him not to be able to move. Strike made his way back down to the field.

As Strike stepped back onto the field, Slithor rose from the ground, having healed from his wounds, mad as all hell. Slithor threw Oblivion's arm at Strike with a growl and great aim. Strike turned and slashed the arm in two with one of his swords. Slithor used the distraction to go on the offensive once again, coming close to Strike and attempted to bite his neck. Strike flung his hand out and grabbed Slithor around the neck, spinning him around and around like a tornado. He threw Slithor up in the air and shot him with a white energy blast, causing one of Slithor's arms and lower body to vaporize, causing too much damage for him to regenerate for at least a few days.

Dr. Syclonus, having gotten the data he needed and being the last Shadow Dragon soldier of Dark Strike's standing, charged at Strike like a leopard. Strike dodged each of his claw attacks. One of Dr. Syclonus's claws cut Strike's chest. Strike brought his hand up to his chest and came away with blood, noticing that he had been cut.

Dr. Syclonus circled him, chuckling, and said, "Your assumption is correct. My claws are made of Divinium, so if you know what's good for you, you'll be more CAREFUL."

Using the last word as a battle cry, Dr. Syclonus lunged at him, and Strike did everything he could to avoid his claws. When he swiped at Strike, he left his face unprotected. Strike then sent a punch at the opening, but he blocked it. Dr. Syclonus shot a high kick at Strike's face, but he did a backflip to avoid the impact, sending his foot to smack into Dr. Syclonus's face. The impact of Strike's foot sent him flying, and he managed to do a flip and landed in a kneeling position. After Strike recovered from the backflip and landed near Dr. Syclonus, he growled, and Strike used his hand to gesture for him to come get him. The doctor charged at Strike again.

Sanus rose from the ground, finally recovered enough from his knockout to join in the fight. Noticing that Dr. Syclonus and Strike were busy fighting each other, he donned a psychotic grin and formed his arm into a rocket launcher. Sanus aimed and locked the missile onto Strike. Dr. Syclonus managed to throw Strike to the ground as the missile was fired.

Strike noticed the missile first and said, "See ya!"

He then teleported away. Noticing the missile too late, Dr. Syclonus turned and saw it.

He said, "Oh sh—" and got blown up by the missile.

When Sanus saw the explosion, he winced and said, "Oh… didn't see that coming. Well at least I got that dragon too."

Strike appeared behind him and said, "You were saying?"

Sanus turned in shock and had no time to react before Strike slammed him headfirst into the field so hard it created a crater. Dark Strike watched the fighting in angry silence. The scene shows each Shadow Dragon burned, blown up, damaged beyond repair, and passed out.

After realizing that the Shadow Dragons sent an army to distract the Dragon Knights and keep them away from Strike, Wingsavior sent Rose and a few other Dragon Knights back to Earth to protect humans from the Shadow Dragons. They tracked Strike in Qualcomm Stadium and arrived right as Dark Strike began to walk toward him. Rose went running to Strike's aide, but Jetfrost grabbed her shoulder and told her not to interfere. Rose got angry and began to argue with Jetfrost about their orders. Jetfrost continued to hold her back and told her they should wait and see what happens. Rose already felt guilty enough about Kira's parents and is on edge, watching Dark Strike and Strike's fierce battle.

Dark Strike walked toward Strike and angrily shouted, "Well, if you want to kill someone right, you kill them yourself!"

Dark Strike rushed toward Strike with his cape flowing in the wind behind him, and Strike also rushed toward Dark Strike; and they both collided into each other with their fists, causing a shock wave and an extreme burst of energy that threw them both backward. As soon as Strike collected himself, he began to run toward Dark Strike with supersonic speed. He went into a butterfly twist move, and while there, he tried to kick Dark Strike with a swift kick to the left side of his face. Dark Strike, moving quickly, did a backflip, kicking Strike's leg and making him spin out of control. Strike, landing on the ground on all fours, regained his composure. He began running back toward Dark Strike with his supersonic speed, punching left and right. However, Dark Strike was able to return the same blows back at Strike with the same velocity of speed. They both were taking a lot of blows to the face and appeared to be evenly matched. As Strike threw one last punch, Dark Strike was able to grab ahold of his fist, crushing it. After a long time of fighting, Strike can't seem to take Dark Strike down.

Dark Strike revealed to Strike, "After I kill you, I plan to blow up the stadium and eventually destroy the planet."

Dark Strike grabbed him by the neck, punched him in the torso and face, and choke slammed him, making him lay motionless on the ground. Dark Strike believed that this is the end of the battle, and he tried to kill Strike by summoning a sword out of dark smoke.

Right as the blade would have come down on Strike's chest, a mass of water came, smacking Dark Strike out of the way. The water revealed itself as Rose with the other Dragon Knight warriors—Jetfrost, Borian, Volt, and Ferrous not far behind. The rest of Kira's friends focused on evacuating the rest of the innocents from the stadium. Rose picked Strike up and flew him to safety as the other Dragon Knights fought off Dark Strike. The rest of Kira's friends fled the stadium.

Jack and Chuck had to hold Mia back as she screamed out, "Strike!"

The other Dragon Knights stood by as Rose flew out after sending wave after wave of attack at Dark Strike, who was trying to recover from being knocked down. Each attack caused Dark Strike to keep hitting a foundational wall of the stadium. The last attack threw him into the wall so hard that he caused half the stadium to crumble on top of him. With that, the Dragon Knights followed Rose. When Dark Strike realized that Strike was gone, he powered up and used his rage to slam both of his claws on the ground, which caused the rest of the stadium to start to crumble around them.

Strike woke up on Dragza. Borian and Ferrous were in the room. Strike didn't recognize them. He had no idea if they were good or bad, and he couldn't remember seeing them at the fight. He jumped out of bed and immediately got in a fighting stance.

Strike began yelling, "Who are you? Where am I? What's going on?"

Borian tried to talk him down and tell him that they aren't his enemies.

Strike was suspicious and yelled, "How am I supposed to know that? Where am I? Where are my friends?"

Rose glided through the doors. Her face curved in an amused smile as she crossed her arms in front of her chest at Strike's fighting stance. He looked at her and he remembered seeing her through his blurred vision at the stadium moments before he blacked out.

Dropping his hands to his sides in wonder, he said, "I know... you."

Rose raised an eyebrow and responded, "Do you?"

He nodded and sat on the edge of the bed. He looked down at his feet and said, "You were at the stadium. You saved me from Dark Strike's sword. You...saved my life." Looking up at Rose, he searched her face and continued, "What I can't figure out is why."

Rose uncrossed her arms in surprise and said, "You really don't know?"

Strike shook his head and brought his hand up to scratch the back of his head.

In confusion, he said, "Uhm, know what?"

Rose's eyes widened, and her mouth dropped open. "You really have no idea?"

Strike's eyes narrowed with more confusion, and he turned to Borian and Ferrous. "What is she talking about?"

They shrugged, and Rose grabbed Strike's hand and pulled him out of the room. Borian shook his head with a chuckle and Ferrous rolled his eyes, shutting the door to the bedroom and following Rose and Strike down the hallway. She led Strike into the larger part of the castle, not giving him time to look at any of the artifacts on display in the hallway.

After several minutes of walking, they came to a large hall (later revealed to be the Hall of History), where the rest of the Dragon Knights are. As they passed the other Dragon Knights, they bowed and paid their respects to Strike, which only confused him more. He tried to ask Rose about it, but she only shushed him and told him one question at a time. As they approached the throne on the far side of the room, Strike saw an old Dragon Knight sitting in a hovering chair near the throne.

Rose released his wrist from her iron grip and called out, "Brother Wingsavior!"

Strike rubbed the area of his wrist that Rose had just released, wincing at the slight pain. He looked around, genuinely intrigued at his surroundings, wondering where on Earth a castle this big could be located.

Wingsavior floated down to the ground and answered Strike's question. "We are not on planet Earth. We are on Planet Dragza." At Strike's startled reaction, Wingsavior added, "No, I can't read minds. Only reactions."

Taking a step back in disbelief, Strike looked from Wingsavior to Rose and back. "Wait, what now? I'm on another PLANET?"

Rose shrugged apologetically and Wingsavior nodded, smiling. Wingsavior walked over to Strike and explained that they had to remove him from the planet Earth or Dark Strike would have destroyed it and everyone he cared about.

"Don't worry, we have Dragzarians watching over your friends to help keep them safe." He put his hand on Strike's shoulder and told him, "Brother, let me show you our Planet Dragza before we say anything more."

Wingsavior guided him to the landing and allowed him to gaze upon Dragza for the first time. When Strike gazed at Dragza, his super eyesight kicked in, and he was able to see hover cars, advanced technology, and even individual Dragzarians of all ages. One Dragzarian woman, in particular, was manipulating water and turning it into rain clouds to water her garden. Another used his powers to shoot fire from his mouth and form Fire Dragons for an audience. Strike was amazed at the Planet Dragza.

He began to tell Wingsavior, "I need to get to Earth to protect my people."

Wingsavior began to tell him that they were hoping to bring Dark Strike to Dragza, so they could protect Strike.

One of the Dragon Knight scouts rushed in to report to Wingsavior. The scout reports to Wingsavior that he has an urgent message from Dark Strike from Earth. All the Dragon Knights gathered together in their meeting room to hear the message. As they all gathered, the room began to transform into a war room with lots of technology. In the center, there appeared a holographic projection of

Dark Strike on the screen. Dark Strike was telling them that Strike Dragon had better return to Earth, or he will start destroying everything on it.

Dark Strike told Strike, "You have seventy-two hours to return, or the destruction begins." Dark Strike turned, swishing his cape, and added, "I will be seeing you soon, brother." He then exploded the hologram that was projecting his message. The picture on the hologram disappeared.

Strike told Wingsavior, "I have to get back to Earth."

Wingsavior responded, "First, we have to get you trained and ready to battle Dark Strike."

Leon Dragon appeared to Strike, telling him, "Listen to Wingsavior. He will help you with whatever you need to get stronger. Don't worry about your friends right now. A week's time on Dragza is equal to a day on Earth, so I need you to concentrate on training."

Wingsavior said, "Strike, you need not to worry. I have soldiers making sure your friends are safe. I am sorry for what happened to your parents, and we will guard them with everything we have. We will fight to protect them even if it kills us. We need you to take down Dark Strike if either of our worlds are to survive."

Strike thought about what Leon said as he looked at Wingsavior and the other Dragon Knights all together then looked around at Dragza and how beautiful a place it is. Strike, while balling up his fists in determination, made his decision.

Looking at Wingsavior, Strike told him, "I will do it! I will train with you! I will take down Dark Strike to not only protect Dragza, but the whole Multiverse. Let's get started."

Wingsavior turned to Strike, and moving his bull staff and pointing the way, stated, "Lead the way, commander."

Strike paused and turned toward Wingsavior and asked him, "Commander?"

Wingsavior patted his shoulder and told him, "Leon Dragon was our commander and leader, and you, Strike Dragon, hold his Spirit Core within you, making you our new commander and leader. However, you are also our KING!"

Strike, thinking to himself, began to ask Wingsavior, "So what am I to you guys? Commander, leader, or king?"

Wingsavior explained, "Our brother! Now then, let me introduce you to our fellow brothers and sister. You have already met our sister, Rose Dragon. She is the one who saved your life."

Rose gave Strike a friendly nod as if to say hi.

Wingsavior introduced him to Blazer Dragon.

Blazer said, "Hey brother! My name is Blazer, and I am the Dragon of Fire," while producing a fireball in the palm of his hand.

Rose, being the Dragon of Water, put out Blazer's fireball. Strike laughed.

Blazer looked at Rose and said, "Hey, you did that on purpose."

Everyone laughed.

Next was Jetfrost. He bent down and froze the water Rose had splashed on Blazer, temporarily freezing him.

He looked at Strike and said, "My name is Jetfrost Dragon. As you can see, I freeze things."

Blazer piped in, saying, "You're enjoying this, aren't you?"

Jetfrost replied, "A little…"

Then came a strong whirlwind as another one of the dragons came forward, saying, "Me next, me next," while spinning his nunchuks to create the wind. "I am Borian Dragon." Getting close to Strike, he whispered to him, "I am the Dragon of Wind."

Strike responded, "Well, that's cool."

Borian Dragon, while chuckling, pointed to Strike and said, "I like him! He gets me!"

Out of nowhere, a lightning bolt flashed across the room and bounced off the wall, coming back and hitting Borian in the ass.

He jumped up and said, "Hey, what was that for, Volt?"

Volt replied, "I was showing off like everyone else. Sorry your ass got in the way. Hi, Strike. I am Volt Dragon." He gave Strike a fist bump with sparks flying.

Finally, the last dragon walked in holding his lab jacket tight, revealing his hand to shake Strike's. Instead of hand, he revealed a mace weapon.

"Hi, Strike. I am Ferrous Dragon."

He realized he had his weapon out instead of his hand. He shook it till he was able to produce his hand to shake Strike's.

Strike said, "How did you do that?"

Ferrous explained, "Its simple"—turning his hand into a hammer then into a flamethrower—"I am the Dragon of Metal and can transform into all kinds of weaponry."

Borian whispered to Strike, "Not only that, but he is the tech head of the family."

Ferrous, hearing what Borian said, turned his other hand that was the flamethrower into a sledgehammer and whacked him in the head.

Borian, being dazed, said, "Twinkle, twinkle little stars," while collapsing to the floor.

Strike looked at Ferrous a little confused and then looked back at Borian.

Ferrous replied, "He is the knucklehead of the family!"

Strike acknowledged, saying, "Oohh."

Wingsavior said, "I am the Dragon of the Earth. Not only of the Earth but also of magic."

Strike questioned him, "Magic?"

Wingsavior responded, "More like," as he raised his hand and then lowered it to the ground, revealing a magical symbol. The symbol lit up, and he summoned a magical winged creature made of rock. After the winged creature was behind Wingsavior, he looked at Strike and said, "That's Dragzarian Magic."

Strike said, "That is unreal."

Wingsavior told Strike, "Now that you have met your brothers and sister of the Dragon Knights, let us begin your training. We have a lot to accomplish in a little bit of time."

Strike and the other Dragon Knights trained to work as a team. They trained him for days. He learned a lot from his brothers and sister. He was able to hone his skills and powers that each of them possessed. Strike, while training, learned of his elemental power. The Power of the Light is the strongest of all eight elements combined.

Leon Dragon appeared to him one day while he was training. Leon was proud of how advanced he had become in his Light Powers.

He explained to Strike that the one element that could rival the light is darkness.

Strike asked Leon, "You are talking about Dark Strike, aren't you?"

Leon explained to him how Dark Strike had become so powerful. A long time ago, Dark Strike was one of the brothers of the Dragon Knights. He was called Obsidion Dragon. His power was Dark Crystal Shadows. He was one of the greatest Dragon Knights that fought in the war against the Shadow Dragons.

"It is a war that we have been fighting through the ages. It is a battle between good and evil. A war between darkness and light. My son, Obsidion, lost the love of his life due to all the fighting. He became bitter and all he cared about was power. The evil corrupted his Shadow Core, and he became the ruler of the Shadow Dragons. He committed genocide of all the Holy Dragons of Light, not realizing that each were able to transfer their powers to me. I was the only one remaining."

Strike, upon hearing this, said, "You were the only Light left?"

Leon turned, facing him, and said, "Yes, I was the only Light left. Before they could take my Spirit Core, I locked it in a crystal and cast it into space. That is the Spirit Core that you now possess. That is why Dark Strike wants to destroy you."

Strike, hearing all this, asked Leon, "Why didn't you destroy Obsidion?"

Leon explained, "Being his father, I couldn't destroy my own son. However, I did defeat him and threw him into the Pit of Darkness. That was the last time I saw him, or so I thought until he returned as Dark Strike, the leader of the Shadow Dragons, or as his minions call him, the Shadow King. His one desire was to destroy me and all of Dragza in order to be the ruler of the Multiverse. You, my son, possessing all the Holy Dragon's Light Powers, are the one true Dragon Knight King who can defeat Dark Strike and bring peace to the Multiverse. For you are the last of the light!"

After hearing all of what Leon said, Strike finally realized all his Spirit Core powers and how to call upon them. While training,

Strike became the most powerful Light Dragon that ever existed. He had mastered the Spirit Core abilities.

Strike, upon waking the next day, was feeling anxious. He went to meet with Wingsavior and the others.

As soon as he saw Wingsavior, he told him, "Now I am really needing to get back to Earth."

Wingsavior turned and tapped his bull staff on the ground with a look of concern on his face. He began explaining to Strike, "I don't think you are ready."

Strike, with a shocked look on his face, asked Wingsavior, "What? What do you mean I am not ready?"

Wingsavior explained further, "The reason we were training you is so you can become a Super Dragon."

Strike replied, "So what more do I need to do to become one?"

Wingsavior walked up to Strike and held up three fingers then explained to him, "There are three options that will get you where you need to be. You need to learn a little more before I feel you will be ready."

Strike replied, "Well, let's get to it because I need to get back to Earth!"

Wingsavior explained, "Option one is to train for one hundred years. Option two is if you learn to feel the true Rage of the Dragon, it will unlock the power from the heart."

Wingsavior looked concerned and paused, causing Strike to be impatient, so he asked, "What-what is the third option?"

Wingsavior gathered his thoughts to tell Strike, "The third option is to feel the pain of loss so severe, that it will trigger you to unleash the power."

Strike replied, "I already lost both of my parents. Wouldn't that be enough to trigger it?"

Wingsavior explained, "You didn't have all the training and experience when that happened. You were not able to call on that power."

Strike replied, "I will take option two. I need to learn to feel the True Rage of the Dragon. Just the thought of Dark Strike going after my sister should be enough."

Volt jumped into the conversation, explaining, "Even if that is true, we need to be sure before you step into battle. Besides, if you engage Dark Strike, you will fail and the Multiverse will be his."

Strike turned and replied, "I don't care what happens to me! I don't care if I am the chosen one or not. I have to get back to Earth to save my family I left behind and all my friends."

Volt replied, "Do you realize how crazy you just got? Even if you want to save Earth, you are the key to save everyone in the Multiverse, not just Earth. As King of the Dragons, surely you would know."

Strike, slamming his fists on the table, yelled, "I would give my life to save everyone, including Dragza, but Earth must come first." Strike gave a heavy sigh and continued, "Look, I may be the King of all Dragons but a true king, no, a true leader will do whatever it takes to set things right. Even if it costs me my life. No matter the strength of the evil that wishes to do harm to the Multiverse, I'll be ready to fight to the end for I am Strike Dragon!"

Everyone applauded his response.

Wingsavior, putting his hand on Strike's shoulder, replied, "You are ready, my brother. We will be with you as well until the very end! We're ready when you are!"

Strike, being the King of the Dragons, commanded them, "Dragon Knights, it's Dragon Time!"

He put his hands together to activate the teleportation technique that he had learned from Leon.

He looked at the other Dragon Knights, telling them, "If you want to go with me, you had better grab on! Otherwise, you will have to catch up."

*****

On the news reports, it shows that it has been a couple of days since the incident the stadium. No one is quite sure what exactly happened there. One of the news reporters played a copy of the hologram that Dark Strike sent to Earth, telling them that they have seventy-two hours to turn over Strike Dragon to him, or he will destroy

Earth. The reporter was telling everyone they had twenty-four hours left before Dark Strike was threatening to appear.

Later that afternoon, there was a news break. They were reporting that there were ships that had appeared in the sky. The news media was calling for Strike to appear.

"If anyone knows where he is, PLEASE let him know we drastically need him!"

The newscast lost its signal, and a picture appeared with the ships in the air. Dark Strike appeared in the news feed walking out of a ship.

He explained, "People of Earth, you have twenty-four more hours to produce Strike Dragon, or I will destroy you all."

The Secretary of Defense for the United States came on with a press conference. He started to explain, "The people of Earth do not know who this Strike Dragon is or where he is. However, we will take the necessary steps to protect ourselves against someone like you."

While the Secretary of Defense was talking to the American people, Dark Strike appeared at the conference.

He grabbed the Secretary of Defense by the throat, lifting him in the air, and stated, "You humans really think that you stand a chance against a dragon? I am Dark Strike, and I want Strike Dragon. I know he cares for you humans, so he will appear before the time is up to try to save you."

Dark Strike disappeared as quickly as he appeared, leaving everyone in a state of shock.

The Secretary of Defense pleaded with the American people, "We need Strike Dragon here now! Strike, if you're out there, please help us!" He announced, "Because of the prior incident that happened in California, the military is asking that everyone evacuate the area immediately. Please do so calmly and quickly."

Jack and Mia were watching the news conference with Chuck and Kari and the two Dragzarians that were watching over them. They all agreed that they were not going to evacuate. The Dragzarians reassured them that Strike Dragon was on his way.

Upon hearing this, Chuck stood up from the couch and asked, "How would you know that?"

One of the Dragzarians replied, "I can sense his power coming, and he wouldn't let us down! Just like Dark Strike said, Strike Dragon would not let everyone down. I do sense he is coming back soon."

Chuck began to panic, asking, "Even if it's true, how do we defend ourselves against those creatures?"

Jack stood and stated, "Follow me, Chuck," as Jack went to the bookcase, opening a secret passageway.

Kari, Mia, and Chuck followed him down to a secret room filled with high-tech weaponry.

Jack went over and picked up one of the weapons, saying, "This is my newest invention, a Divinium Blaster. I made this weapon by using parts from their robot drones that attacked Strike. I adjusted it to penetrate their metal."

The others were surprised that Jack was able to develop a weapon like that.

Mia asked Jack, "How long did it take you to make all these?"

Jack replied, "I started making this right after the drones attacked Kira when he was training. I thought they might come in handy, just in case."

Mia told Jack, "We should get these to the military to help out."

Jack responded, "No, I think we should hang on to this to protect ourselves. Not to mention they would have too many questions that we wouldn't be able to answer."

She agreed, although he could tell she was sad.

He asked her, "What's wrong, Mia?"

She replied, "I miss Kira. I really wish he was here to save us."

This was a complete surprise to Chuck and Kari since they had no idea that Strike Dragon and Kira were one and the same! Before they could ask for an explanation, they heard a loud thump. They all ran out of the secret room to the living room, just in time to see a flash outside the window. They also heard a roaring thunder sound outside Jack's house, so they all ran outside to see what was happening. Strike and the Dragon Knights appeared right before their very eyes.

Mia was so excited, she ran up to her brother and gave him a big hug, exclaiming, "Kira! I am so glad you're back. I missed you and thought I would never see you again."

97

He told her, "You could never get rid of me that easily!"

They all laughed.

Jack told him, "That creature has been threatening Earth unless they hand you over to him."

Strike responded, "I have been training on Dragza for weeks. A week on Dragza is like a day on Earth. I've been training on Dragza for a while, and I am ready to battle and take on my brother, Dark Strike. I have a lot to tell you guys, but for now, I need to prepare to take him down before he hurts anybody else. I needed to make sure that you are all safe prior to defeating Dark Strike."

Volt said to him, "Well, what are we waiting for? Let's go kick some butt!"

Jack asked Strike, "Are you going to take us with you?"

Strike told him, "It is better for all of you to stay here, where you will be safe."

Mia piped up, "But we want to go with you!"

Chuck and Kari agreed.

Strike told them, "No, I don't think it will be a good idea."

Jack turned to look at Mia, Chuck, and Kari, giving them a nod with a look and a wink, letting them know he will make sure they get there all on their own. Strike and the Dragon Knights took flight.

Mia, looking at the others, asked them, "Can you believe how my brother just treated us!"

Jack replied, "Yeah, but we're not going to listen to him."

Chapter 12

Strike and the other Dragon Knights headed toward Camp Pendleton Military Base.

Upon arriving, the guards asked them, "Who are you?"

Strike told them, "I am the one the creature Dark Strike is looking for. I am here to take him on. Who's in charge here?"

The guard said, "Follow me and I will take you to him."

Strike and the other Dragon Knights followed the guard to the main headquarters. When they arrived, the Secretary of Defense came out to greet them.

He started to tell Strike, "Boy, am I glad to see you! We had no idea who this Dark Strike was looking for."

Strike told him, "We can handle it from here. You and these other guys may want to evacuate the area. I don't want him to kill any more innocent people."

The Secretary of Defense and the soldiers proceeded to evacuate the area.

As soon as they were all gone, Strike and the other Dragon Knights called out to Dark Strike, saying, "Here we are, Dark Strike! Come and get us if you have the guts!"

Dark Strike appeared before Strike along with his army.

He told Strike, "I thought you weren't going to show up, and I would have to kill all these primates."

Strike angrily replied, "I would not allow you to do that, Dark Strike. These are my people, and I would risk everything I have to protect them." As Strike was saying that, his eyes began to glow with awesome power. He told Dark Strike while raising his fist, "Or die trying."

Dark Strike smirked and said, "How are you going to stop us? Last time we battled, you didn't stand a chance against me."

At that point, Strike raised his hand in the air and fired a powerful energy blast that blew up their ship that was in the air that crashed and exploded into the ocean in a million pieces. Dark Strike had a look of shock on his face. When he turned to look back at Strike, he had a look of rage. Strike raised his hand again and fired an energy blast that knocked Dark Strike off his feet. He was able to deflect the energy blast that Strike had fired from his men.

Dark Strike was angry and told Strike, "You are going to regret doing that to my ship."

Strike responded, "You are going to regret the day you invaded my home and killed my parents. As you know, my powers become stronger when I tap into my anger. I will draw on my Spirit Core power to put an end to you and all your tyranny."

Dark Strike jolted, "We will just have to see about that!" He was unleashing his dark energy, making it sound as if there was an earthquake.

Strike announced to the Dragon Knights, "For the freedom of Earth!" He then looked toward his comrades. "To the Multiverse!"

Dark Strike shouted, "Attack and destroy them all!"

The Shadow Dragons rushed into battle.

Strike turned to look at the Shadow Dragons and powered up his energy as he shouted a final word, "For Dragza!"

The Dragon Knights rushed into battle as well. They charged toward each other and they all collided. It was an intense release of power and energy. The Dragon Knights fought the Shadow Dragons with their weapons made of divinium. They were able to do major damage to the Shadow Dragons. The Dragon Knights were also taking some major damage due to the fact that the Shadow Dragons' weapons were made of Shadow Crystals, the very thing that weakens the Dragon Knights.

Strike and Dark Strike were off to the side of the battle, watching as their soldiers were trying to kill each other. Strike noticed that the Dragon Knights were able to take down some of the Shadow Dragons. Blazer was able to burn about fifty of the Shadow Dragons with his fireballs. When others attacked him from behind, he spun around like a tornado, lifting him in the air full of fire, and was able to burn the Shadow Dragons on the ground.

Jetfrost was standing in the middle of another bunch of Shadow Dragons. When they tried to attack him, he moved with light speed. After passing them all at once, he turned around, and he clapped his hands, and as he did, he froze them all in a solid iceberg.

Jetfrost walked up to the block of ice and said, "You guys are tough but not that tough!" He gripped the iceberg, causing it to disintegrate into a million pieces, turning the Shadow Dragons into snowflakes.

Next up, was Wingsavior. He was in the middle of the battle when one of the largest Shadow Dragons came up to him.

The large Shadow Dragon asked Wingsavior, "You are supposed to be the strongest one of the Dragon Knights?" He burst into laughter. "You are nothing but a puny old man!" He began winding up his shoulder, saying, "This is going to be too easy." He then threw a punch at him.

Wingsavior stopped the giant Shadow Dragon's fist with his hand and crushed it, causing him to scream in agonizing pain. Wingsavior grabbed ahold of him, slamming him on the ground back and forth four times, putting him out of his misery. Wingsavior, noticing he had pieces of the Shadow Dragon on his coat, simply brushed it off.

Turning to the remaining Shadow Dragons, he asked, "Anyone else?"

At that, some of the Shadow Dragons dropped their weapons and began to retreat.

When Wingsavior saw them retreating, he asked, "Where are you running off to?"

He lifted his cane in the air and brought it down with a loud thump, causing what appeared to be an earthquake, causing the ground beneath their feet to crack open and swallow them up. He thumped his cane again and caused the ground to close.

"I may be old, but I AM A DRAGON MASTER!"

More of the Shadow Dragons were heading toward Rose. That is when she used her water attacks to trap them in a sphere.

As she did, Volt appeared with his lightning speed, asking her, "Mind if I help, sis?" while showing his hand electrified.

Rose told Volt, "Go ahead, brother."

Volt, raising his hand, caused a thunder and lightning storm from the sky. As he did, he was able to target the water sphere, causing it to electrocute all the Shadow Dragons in it.

After he and Rose were able to kill all the Shadow Dragons in the sphere, she told him, "Nice shot!"

He responded, "Hey, thanks for giving me the opportunity!"

The two of them began to chuckle before noticing more Shadow Dragons coming toward them.

They both stood back to back, and Volt told her, "You take the one hundred on the right, and I will take the one hundred on the left."

She said, "I COULD just take them ALL!"

Volt responded, "You are always trying to have all the fun! You have to learn to share."

Rose replied, "No, YOU'RE the one always trying to steal all the fun."

Volt told her, "You know what…touché!"

Volt, powering up and with lightning speed, threw lightning bolts and caused the one hundred Shadow Dragons he was attacking to explode. Rose, using a water whip, started charging toward the Shadow Dragons as one of them tried to throw a punch at her. She grabbed him by the arm and did a judo flip and stomped him, breaking his neck. She then put the remaining Shadow Dragons back into a sphere.

Looking at Volt, she stated, "Okay, bro! Go ahead! Light 'em up with all you got!"

Volt then electrocuted them all.

Looking back at Rose, he said, "You're the best, sis!"

She gave him a thumbs-up. Another Shadow Dragon began to charge at Volt.

Rose reacted by warning him, "Watch out!" As she turned her water whip into a trident, she threw it and stabbed the Shadow Dragon.

When Volt saw the Shadow Dragon that she stabbed, he turned to her and said, "Thanks!"

Out of nowhere, a juggernaut Shadow Dragon pulled up a sledgehammer-type weapon to slam her with.

Volt, in turn, told her, "Look out, sis!"

When she turned, it looked like it was too late for her to dodge. Before the hammer was about to hit her, all of a sudden, a laser shot the juggernaut through the heart, causing it to collapse to the ground. She turned quickly to see who fired the laser at the juggernaut and saw Jack standing there with a big old grin on his face.

Jack replied, "That was cool!"

She asked Jack, "What are you doing here?"

He replied, "Saving your butt!"

Volt arrived, telling Jack, "Nice gun."

He replied, "Thanks! I made this from a few parts from the drones a while back."

Rose told Jack, Mia, Chuck, and Kari, "Take cover and let us battle these guys!"

Jack reacted by stating, "No problem. We got your back!"

They all stood with blasters locked and loaded. Sixty juggernaut Shadow Dragons charged toward them. Rose and Volt were preparing to protect Jack and his friends. The Shadow Dragons were caught by a hurricane, pulling them off the ground and sending them to the sky. It revealed a spinning nunchuck, and it was Borian.

He said, "Sorry we're late! We had to take care of the Shadow Dragons from the eastside! But we're here now."

Ferious said, "You guys go on ahead! We've got this covered."

Borian asked Ferious, "Well, bro, you think you can take the shot?"

They looked at every one of the Shadow Dragons in the sky.

Ferious analyzed them, then popped his knuckles, and said, "Oh yeah! I got this!"

Using his Metal Core Powers, he slammed his hands to the ground, forming liquid metal and shaping it into a weapon of his choice—a giant gun turret.

As Ferious got on it, he aimed at one of the Shadow Dragons and said, "Let there be fireworks!"

He pressed the button on the gun turret, shooting a thousand rounds at them in the sky. As they were shot, they exploded like fireworks. Ferious hopped off the turret to meet up with Borian.

They high-fived each other as Borian said, "Nice job, Bro!"

Ferious replied, "I knew you would like those fireworks."

As they were enjoying the fireworks, a stealthy Shadow Dragon was about to attack both of them until Borian elbowed it on the face, thus breaking its nose, and it bled to death.

Ferious said to Borian, "How did you know there was a Shadow Dragon behind us?"

Borian explained, "I didn't."

Meanwhile, Strike and Dark Strike were sizing each other up as Dark Strike knew that the Shadow Dragons are losing the battle, even though they outnumbered the Dragon Knights.

He told Strike, "I take it you've heard the story about my past?"

Strike replied, "Yeah, Leon told me everything. So tell me, why would you do this to your own family?"

He replied, "You mean the same family who denied me of my destiny? The same family who let the love of my life die? The same family who sentenced me to death and banished me like an outcast?"

Strike explained, "You brought this on yourself, and because of your recklessness, you have become the very monster that not even your loved one would acknowledge."

Dark Strike's aura was powering up with evil energy and he told Strike, "Let's finish this!"

When Dark Strike said that, he and Strike were in a standoff. They pulled out their weapons. Dark Strike summoned his sword with the snap of his finger. It appeared with a dark, black aura around it. When Strike pulled the two swords from behind his back, both were glowing with light. They both glared at each other, eye to eye. About the same time, a weapon from the others battling came flying in their direction. It triggered them to attack each other. When their swords clashed, it caused a massive explosion that created a shock wave that caused the Shadow Dragons to be pushed back and sent them flying. Fortunately, Wingsavior created an earth-like wall, shielding the Dragon Knights, Jack, and his friends from the shock wave, so they were able to stand their ground.

When the shock wave ended, Strike and Dark Strike were battling with their swords with epic proportions the whole time. Their battle got so intense, they wound up on top of the tallest building. When Kari saw them crash over on the building, she thought it could be her chance to help Strike. Without Jack and Mia noticing, she hopped in the jeep and drove to where they were. Kari didn't realize it, but Chuck had also jumped on board. The battle was so severe, there was nothing but dust and smoke.

When Kari arrived, she rushed inside the building to try to get to where Strike and Dark Strike were battling. She couldn't take the elevators because they weren't working. She instead took the stairs. Chuck was trying to catch up with Kari, but he was carrying the heavy weapon, so it took him a little longer. When Kari arrived on the roof, she saw them in standoff poses, trying to sum up what their next move would be.

Dark Strike smirked at Strike and said, "Not bad! You're a lot stronger than I thought you'd be."

Strike replied, "I hold all the powers of the Spirit Core and been trained by the Dragon Knights on Dragza to defeat you. Why don't you give up, so I don't have to destroy you, my brother?"

Dark Strike chuckled and said, "You know it's not going to be that easy! I have no heart. I despise my Dragon Knight brothers. I wish for nothing more than to destroy them all, including you!" His sword began to glow with a bright-red aura of hatred.

Strike sighed and said, "If that's the way you want it!" Strike's swords were glowing as bright as the sun as he powered them up. He then crossed his arms with them, stating, "Then so be it!"

With a thunderous battle cry, he and Dark Strike charged toward each other. When they clashed, another explosion of a shock wave caused the windows of the building to shatter and fall. Kari ducked down when she saw the shock wave coming. When Chuck felt the building shaking, he held onto the railing of the stairs to secure himself.

When the building quit shaking, he looked up and yelled, "Kari!"

He dropped the heavy weapon and ran upstairs to see if she was okay. She luckily was able to dodge the shock wave. As she stood up, she saw nothing but a cloud of smoke. When the smoke and dust cleared, both Strike and Dark Strike were still both standing. Strike's swords had taken some damage, and Dark Strike was left holding nothing but the handle of his sword. Dark Strike now realized his sword was destroyed. He chuckled and tossed the remaining handle aside.

He took his hand and clutched it into a fist and said, "You've done well with your swords, but how are you at martial arts?"

Strike nodded and dropped his swords to the ground, taking on the dragon pose to begin to battle.

Meanwhile, Kari found a hiding place just in case another shock wave was to take place. From where she hid, she could witness their standoff. They were anticipating the other's move. A part of a broken window fell to the floor and the battle began.

Dark Strike attempted a front kick and missed. Strike then landed a straight left to Dark Strike's face, stunning him momentarily and sending him back several feet. Strike charged at Dark Strike with a left-right front punch and roundhouse, knocking him to the ground. When Dark Strike gathered himself and got on his feet, Strike attempted a high leg kick that just missed connecting the top of Dark Strike's head. Dark Strike then connected with a right backhand punch that sent Strike flying into a support beam. Strike gathered his senses and charged back at Dark Strike, creating the two of them to meet in a power struggle, causing a brief stalemate and making it seem like an earthquake. Strike gained the upper hand, pushing Dark Strike to the edge of the building.

Dark Strike said while chuckling, "Not bad, dragon! You really have gotten stronger since our last battle, so there's no reason for me to hold back after all!"

Strike responded, "What's that?"

Dark Strike revealed his true power, a dark energy aura that made the top half of the building crumble. Dark Strike then head-butted Strike and uppercut him to the stomach, sending him back. Strike clenched his midsection from the blow while Dark Strike charged at him with a clawed open hand. Strike managed to grab a piece of a desk that shielded the attempted clawing by Dark Strike, allowing him to connect a fierce punch to Dark Strike's face. He then repaid Dark Strike with an uppercut to the stomach of his own and clawed Dark Strike on the face and left side.

Dark Strike managed to grab Strike by the throat and shouted, "You dare to damage me like no one ever has before!"

Dark Strike then left punched Strike to the face three times and tossed him into a pile of debris. Strike struggled to get to his feet, but Dark Strike was able to pin him down on top of the pile of debris. Strike attempted to free himself, but the power of Dark Strike's foot on top of him was too great.

While Dark Strike had Strike pinned, he said, "You did pretty well considering no one else has ever been able to damage me until now! The truth be told, you and I are not so different. We are both kings that should rule the Multiverse."

Strike responded, "I am nothing like you! You are a monster who takes the lives of the innocent!"

Dark Strike grinned and said, "Sure you are!" Dark Strike grabs Strike's horns and continued, "You just don't know it yet!" Dark Strike then rips Strike's horns from his head.

Strike lets out a scream of agony.

Meanwhile, Kari witnessing it all unfold, tried to work up the gun to fire at Dark Strike. Dark Strike took one of the horns and stabbed Strike in the left hand and stomped his right hand, causing Strike's further agony.

Dark Strike then prepared to stab Strike in the heart with the other horn, saying, "Farewell, brother, for you will not live to see me as the ruler of the Multiverse!"

Just then, an energy laser blast hit Dark Strike in the back that Kari managed to fire. Dark Strike's cape was half destroyed by the blast, and his back was also burned. He turned in the direction of where the blast came from, noticing it was from Kari. His eyes became crimson red from his rage.

Dark Strike said, "You…you insect!"

Strike, also noticing Kari, then said her name in a weak voice.

Meanwhile, Chuck has arrived at the scene. He saw Kari is the one who shot Dark Strike. He noticed Dark Strike realize she is the one who did it also.

Dark Strike said to her, "Well, for a primate, you shoot pretty well! But let me ask you something…" Dark Strike then lifted the remaining horn into the air and said to her, "Can you dodge THIS?"

As Dark Strike prepared to throw the horn at Kari, Strike yelled, "Dark Strike, don't!"

Dark Strike launched the horn with the aim directly toward her heart. Chuck then jumped between Kari and the approaching horn with the horn stabbing him in the chest instead. Chuck immediately hits the ground, causing Kari to scream and drop the gun.

"Chuck!"

Strike, in disbelief, said, "Chuck…no! This can't be happening! It just can't be!"

Thoughts popped into Strike's head about when his parents were murdered. He felt enormous rage come over him and his heart-beat nearly out of his chest. The Spirit Core inside him was growing with a glowing light energy force.

Dark Strike approached Chuck lying on the ground with Kari comforting him and said, "I never knew humans could love each other enough to do that… It almost touches my heart…except I don't have a heart to begin with!" Dark Strike then said to Kari, "Don't feel bad because I can easily allow you to join him"—He extended his claws on one hand and prepared to swipe her—"…in the afterlife!"

As his arm started downward, Strike grabbed his arm with a mighty grip.

Dark Strike then said to Strike with a chuckle, "So you wish to fight some more, do you? As much as I would like to, I have a couple of weak humans to slay…"

With that, Strike's grip became so intense, it crushed Dark Strike's wrist! Dark Strike screamed with horrid agony. He managed to pull free and punched Strike in the face with his good hand, noticing it didn't faze Strike one bit.

In amazement, he said, "How can that be with the might I put in that punch? How are you still standing?"

Strike responded, "First, you killed my parents…then there were all the innocent people at the football stadium and the park ranger… Now, you killed my best friend… For what you've done, YOU MUST PAY!"

Suddenly, a beam of light shot from Strike's body, illuminating the sky, causing clouds to appear along with thunder and lightning, shaking the entire city as if an earthquake was taking place. Everyone in attendance stood in amazement at what was happening. Wingsavior, using his elemental powers, levitated the people above the ground to keep them from being injured.

Mia, in a daze of confusion, asked, "What is going on?"

Blazer asked, "Strike is doing this, isn't he?"

Wingsavior responded by saying, "Yes, that would be him!"

Rose said to Wingsavior, "I… I just can't believe this is happening!"

Mia responded to Rose, "What is this we are witnessing, Rose?"

Wingsavior stepped forward to explain, "Strike has unleashed the incredible!"

Mia, still in need of more clarification, said, "What do you mean by the incredible, Wingsavior?"

He responded, "He has reached the power of Super Dragon!"

All of a sudden, Strike's skin changed from the silver color it was to a white, diamond-like sparkle. His torso changed in color from red to yellow, and his armor went from blue to silver with gold lightning bolt designs. His horns grew back as smaller versions than previously and shaped like lightning bolts instead. His mask no longer existed, exposing his entire face. His eyes changed from yellow to sapphire blue. His pants went from their original black color to metallic blue. The previous symbol on his back that meant light changed to the symbol of "miracles." The light from the sky faded and revealed him fully transformed.

Meanwhile, Dark Strike stood in amazement at the transformation of Strike. Strike then turned to Dark Strike's direction and held out his arm in preparation for the final battle. A massive force was released from Strike's palm toward Dark Strike that sent him flying and smashing him into an entirely different building. Strike then turned his attention toward Kari and Chuck. He went on his knee to console Kari and try to revive Chuck without success.

Chuck managed to grab his wrist, saying, "It's okay, Strike. You've done all you can do."

Strike sadly responded, "But I can't bear to see you go out like this!"

With a grin, Chuck responded, "I know you tried, but this looks like the end of the road for me."

Meanwhile, Kari was weeping uncontrollably.

Chuck then placed his hand on Kari's face and began to confess, "I have loved you from the first time we met, and I wanted you to know that, Kari."

She responded, "I'm glad you finally told me, Chuck, because I, too, love you."

Chuck coughed up blood and said, "Strike, I'd like one last request."

Strike responded, "Anything you'd like, Chuck."

Chuck, with his final request, said, "Please take good care of Kari for she has always had feelings for you and take down Dark Strike. You have a multiverse to save!"

Strike grabbed Chuck's hand and said, "Don't worry, Chuck, you have my word on that!"

With that, Chuck took his last breath and closed his eyes for the final time. Strike, noticing there's no more rise and fall of Chuck's chest, realized his friend is no longer with them. Strike took Chuck's hands and placed them together across his chest. He stood up and told Kari to remain with Chuck while he proceeded to go deal with Dark Strike. Kari witnessed Strike hover above the ground and take on a glowing, white, cosmic-like energy and bursted in the direction of Dark Strike, causing a sonic boom.

Meanwhile, Dark Strike has been trying to free himself from being embedded in the wall Strike sent him flying into. Suddenly, Dark Strike noticed a blurring, glowing light-headed in his direction. He realized it was Strike returning to battle. He attempted to shoot an energy blast toward Strike, but he dodged the force and continued his charge.

Dark Strike yelled, "You son of a…"

Dark Strike continued to fire at Strike to no avail as Strike dodged every one of the blasts. Strike managed to reach Dark Strike with a resounding battle cry and punched Dark Strike in the face with such a force, it sends Dark Strike flying through five buildings. Strike and Dark Strike wind up in the middle of the street from the impact that caused a deep crater.

Strike stood over Dark Strike and asked, "Is that the limit to your power, brother? I'm kind of disappointed!"

Dark Strike, with glowing eyes, responded, "You don't know the half of my true power!"

Dark Strike then unleashed an obsidian dark crystal power upon Strike that he avoided by doing a backflip. Meanwhile, Dark Strike managed to get to his feet and continued to unleash the deadly power toward Strike. Strike managed to dodge them all, catching the last one before it could do him damage, crushing it like it was nothing in his hand. Dark Strike's amazement turned to frustration at what Strike was able to do with the crystal.

Dark Strike, in a most demonic voice, said, "This is not possible! How is it that you are stronger than me?"

Strike responded, "Because unlike you, Dark Strike, my might is for the good of others, and that takes me to a whole other level!"

With that, Dark Strike changed into a demonic aura of red and black and shouted, "Damn you, Strike Dragon! I am Lord Dark Strike, ruler of the Multiverse, the Shadow King! I will not be bested by a mere human who thinks he's a dragon!"

Dark Strike initiated a fierce charge at Strike with claws exposed, only for Strike to evade his every move with blocks and pivots. Dark

Strike's attack is so extreme, he missed Strike and claws a vehicle, shredding it in half. Dark Strike managed to get behind Strike and prepared to attack him from behind. Strike turned immediately and was able to catch Dark Strike's wrist in midair, taking him by surprise with the move.

"My turn," Strike said in a calm and collected voice.

Still holding Dark Strike's wrist with one hand, he unleashed an epic punch to Dark Strike's torso with the other. The punch is such that it sent Dark Strike airborne with Strike right behind him as if he was being teleported. Strike gave Dark Strike a roundhouse kick to the rib cage, causing blood to spew from his mouth and sending him crashing to Earth. As Dark Strike gathered himself and tried to punch Strike, Strike blocked the punch and began a rapid punch sequence to Dark Strike's face and stomach. The punches were so devastating, they penetrated Dark Strike's armor. With a final upper-cut to the abdomen, Strike lifts Dark Strike by one of his horns to reveal Dark Strike took severe damage.

Barely conscious, Dark Strike muttered in agony while cough-ing up blood, "Is this how it all ends, Strike…by killing me? You fool, even if you do, there will always be another force far stronger than me to take my place."

Strike responded with a deep sigh, "Do you actually think I wish to kill you, Dark Strike? The son of Leon Dragon and like a brother to me and my siblings? You may not see it, but I see a second chance for you…" He then offered his hand to Dark Strike in truce. "Give up your evil ways, Dark Strike, and return to the side of the Dragon Knights where you belong."

Dark Strike, realizing that he could be sincere, in return, offered his hand but with hesitation. Suddenly, the darkness that overpowers Dark Strike took over and he slapped Strike's hand away.

"I will not go back to the Dragon Knights' side! You think you can change what I am with mere words? I'm not going back! I like being Dark Strike! It's who I am now! Now and forever!"

Strike's fist clenched so tightly you can hear the knuckles crack. His eyes started to glow a cosmic-blue color.

Strike added, "I'm sorry that you're making that choice, brother!"

Strike then thumped Dark Strike's forehead, sending him flying and skimming through the pavement. When Dark Strike came to a stop, he was partially buried in the ground. Strike turned and walked away to the cheers of the others who just witnessed the epic battle.

Blazer yelled, "Yes! Way to go, Strike!"

Volt chimed in, "That's our bro!"

Jack added, "That's the might of a hero!"

Rose yelled, "Yahoo!"

Mia appeared to be happy until she noticed Wingsavior being unamused.

She said, "What's wrong, Wingsavior?"

With a troubled look on his face, he responded, "I don't think this is the end."

Borian said, "What do you mean, Wingsavior?"

Jetfrost interjected, "I'm with Wingsavior. I sense it too!"

Ferious asked, "You mean you notice it too, Jetfrost?"

He nodded in agreement. "Yes, I do!"

Jack asked, "What are you guys talking about?"

Wingsavior explained, "I sense Dark Strike's evil still lurking!"

Borian exclaimed shockingly, "You mean he's not dead?"

Wingsavior, in a sad tone, responded, "I fear he is not."

Everyone then noticed an evil glowing energy presence coming from where Dark Strike came to rest. Strike also noticed what the others noticed, stopped in his tracks to observe what was happening.

He said with a sigh, "Somehow I knew it wouldn't be that easy."

Suddenly, Dark Strike began to rise into the air, taking on the form of a giant dragon. As he transformed, a massive shock wave took place, and darkness overcame the skies. A lightning and thunderstorm appeared out of nowhere. Meanwhile, the transformation is complete with Dark Strike having a tail, wings, and spikes protruding from both of his forearms. His teeth became strong enough to bite through anything. His eyes appeared to be more vicious than ever, like those of a demon. When he came to rest, it felt as though an earthquake was taking place.

After the dust cleared, it revealed Dark Strike in his newfound form. Everyone stood in shock seeing what he'd become. Wingsavior

113

used magic to create a barrier between them and Dark Strike. Strike approached Dark Strike, powering up an aura as he got closer to him. When Strike got close enough, he took on a battle stance. Dark Strike then let go of a mighty roar that was so intense, it caused a sonic boom that shattered glass in buildings for miles. Dark Strike then focused on his attack on Strike. Strike suddenly took off into the air with Dark Strike following him in hot pursuit.

Once in the clouds, they engaged in battle again. When the lightning struck, you could see them battling. At one point, you can see Strike connecting a mighty right punch to Dark Strike's face. At another point, you see Dark Strike's tail whacking Strike about a mile away. Strike managed to stop himself and retaliated with a kick of his own to Dark Strike's midsection, causing blood to once again fly from his mouth. Dark Strike recovered and attempted to attack Strike with open claws to no avail as Strike once again is able to dodge them. Strike managed to catch both wrists, creating a power struggle before Dark Strike used his fire blast from his mouth on him. Strike then powered up his own energy blast from his mouth and unleashed it on Dark Strike. The two forces meet, causing an explosion, sending the two flying in the opposite directions.

Strike is stunned from crashing into a building and managed to come to his knees, but Dark Strike is already in position to do more damage. Dark Strike gripped him in one hand and body slammed him and followed up with a rapid punch session. Dark Strike then used his fire from his mouth once again to hold Strike on the ground, causing an enormous explosion effect. It caused a crater to the point you could no longer see Strike. Dark Strike, feeling that he's killed Strike, lets out a loud roar of victory to the horror of all witnessing the battle.

Mia began to sob uncontrollably, feeling she has lost her brother. Jack is beside her with anger and aimed the blaster gun at Dark Strike's back. Sensing he was about to be blasted, Dark Strike turned around to his surprise and noticed everyone else stood with Jack to do battle.

In a crazed, growling voice, Dark Strike muttered, "Do you all wish to fight me?"

Jack replied, "For Strike Dragon, yes, we do!"

Suddenly, Dark Strike spread his wings and yelled, "Then so be it!"

As he was about to attack, he felt a tug on his tail. He turned to see in amazement that it was Strike holding him back from being able to attack them. Strike, although appearing to be horribly battered and beaten, was still alive and was eager to continue the fight. Everyone was astonished to see Strike had survived what just happened to him.

"He's alive!" Mia is heard shouting with newfound joy.

The others all cheered with total excitement!

Strike, in a spiritual voice, commanded, "You stay away from my friends, Dark Strike! Your battle is with me!"

Strike began spinning while holding onto Dark Strike's tail ever so fast until he released him flying toward the ocean. Meanwhile, Strike teleported himself to the ocean to be there when Dark Strike arrived. As Dark Strike approached, Strike prepared a sledgehammer move and slammed Dark Strike down into the ocean with a huge splash. Dark Strike attempted to resurface but Strike charged him, taking the battle deep beneath the water. Strike battered Dark Strike with an unrelenting pounding until Dark Strike was able to get one punch in. Strike, unfazed by the punch, managed to swim up Dark Strike's arm and kick him in the face with such power, it knocked a tooth out. Strike grabbed Dark Strike by the face and hit him with a powerful cosmic energy blast from his mouth called the Dragon Cannon Blast, causing a catastrophic explosion, parting the sea. Strike managed to come to his feet, holding his arm that was damaged by the explosion, and saw that Dark Strike is nowhere to be found.

Suddenly, a tremor took place, revealing a large, dark figure coming from the ground and going skyward. It was a horribly damaged Dark Strike, just barely clinging to life.

In a faint voice, Dark Strike managed to mutter, "I've had enough of this planet and you as well, Strike! I've decided to put an end to it once and for all with one more shot!"

<del>115</del>

An evil, dark energy sphere gathered in the mouth of Dark Strike, growing ever so immensely.

Dark Strike taunted, "What's the matter, Strike Dragon? Do you not think your super dragon powers can stop this?"

With that, Strike said to himself, "Is there a way I can truly put an end to this? There's got to be a way!"

All of a sudden, he felt a hand on his shoulder and heard a familiar voice that said, "You're not in this alone, Strike."

He recognized the voice of being that of Leon Dragon. He then turned in the direction of where the voice came, and to his surprise, there was Leon.

"You're here to help me?" Strike said in a bewildered voice.

Nodding, Leon responded, "Not only am I here but so are all the others who have gone before you."

Strike noticed all the dragons standing behind Leon. In the crowd, he saw his parents, both having proud looks on their faces. Tears rolled down Strike's face, thinking he would never see them again. Just then, he felt yet another tap on his shoulder. He turned and realized it is Chuck.

"Hey, Kira!"

Strike beamed seeing his lifelong friend is also there.

Strike asked Chuck, "How is it possible for you to be here?"

Chuck responded, "You'll have to ask Leon!"

Leon explained, "Before he died, as with your parents, their souls were saved by the Spirit Core."

Strike asked, "So what can we do to stop Dark Strike?"

Leon then closed his eyes and responded, "There is a way to put an end to this once and for all. If you use the power of the Spirit Core from our ancestor, Torius, the Spirit of the Dragon technique, that would be all we need to defeat Dark Strike."

Strike, with a puzzled look on his face, asked, "How do we do it then?"

Leon Dragon took Strike's damaged arm in his hands and used his healing ability to restore it like new.

"Open up your hand, Strike, and let the energy of the Spirit Core and us do the rest!"

Strike then closed his eyes and concentrated on the Spirit Core and felt its essence and power growing. Leon, meanwhile, allowed himself to become a part of the essence, as well as all the others who accompanied him. All their energy combined transferred into a sphere in Strike's palm. Inside the sphere, there appeared a dragon roaring. An incredible feeling of strength came over Strike with all the combined energy from everyone.

Meanwhile, Dark Strike then said, "It's time for you and this pitiful world to die, Strike!"

Strike responded, "I don't think so, Dark Strike. The only thing that's going to end here is you!"

Dark Strike then fired the ball of energy that has been accumulating in his mouth toward Strike. Strike, with a thunderous takeoff toward the released energy that came from Dark Strike, collided with a massive energy-to-energy power struggle.

The energy from Dark Strike seemed to push Strike backward, causing Dark Strike to shout, "It's over, Strike Dragon! Just give up and accept you and your world's fate!"

Strike, in a bold tone, responded, "That's the difference between you and me, Dark Strike, you may have the power to conquer and rule the Multiverse, but I have something that you don't understand. Something only a true leader would know about. To be a true king, you can't be cruel to others. You treat them like the friends or family they are. Because of that, their strength becomes my strength, and their hope becomes my will. Their spirit becomes my might."

With that, the Spirit Core's glow became ever so bright and pierced through Dark Strike's energy force, causing it to fade away.

Dark Strike, in utter disbelief, yelled, "What? No, this can't be!"

Strike blazed toward Dark Strike and connected the Spirit of the Dragons force, sending them into space.

Strike began, "As you can see, I have a power that you lack, the power of unity!"

Suddenly, all the dragons revealed themselves and commenced a vicious attack on Dark Strike. The attack caused Dark Strike to become consumed by the light. With one final blow, Strike, with the spirit of Leon guiding his hand, connected the sphere with Dark

Strike's face, purifying him and causing him to explode in an ever so bright light.

With a battle cry from both Strike and Leon's spirit, they said, "Your fate is sealed!"

The last words to be heard from Dark Strike were, "Damn you, Strike Dragon!"

Suddenly, the light faded away, all became calm, and the sky was blue once again. Everyone was curious as to whether or not Strike Dragon survived the explosion.

Mia turned to Wingsavior and asked, "Do you think Strike survived that horrible explosion?"

Wingsavior closed his eyes and put his head down and responded, "I don't know, Mia. Let's certainly hope so!"

Just then, Mia looked up and her sorrow immediately turned to jubilation as she saw Strike hovering back down to Earth ALIVE! Everyone rushed over to greet Strike as he came to rest on the ground. Mia wrapped her arms around Strike's neck while being totally concerned about his well-being. Strike embraced her in return, letting her know he was okay.

Borian asked Strike, "Is it over?"

Strike responded, "Yes, it's finally over. Dark Strike is no more."

Everyone cheered with utter excitement! Jack offered Strike a fist bump for a job well done!

Wingsavior said, "Excellent work, Strike! What you've done here today proves you are the mightiest of all protectors!" He then announced to the crowd, "Long live the King!"

Everyone chimed in, "Long live the King! Long live the King!"

Strike, in a modest tone, said, "I so appreciate everyone's gratitude, but I only did what is right. I'm just sorry I couldn't save Dark Strike from his evil ways."

Wingsavior patted Strike on the shoulder and said, "Not even a Dragon King could have! It's all right, Strike. You tried your best!"

Suddenly, something came crashing down from the sky that got everyone's attention. Rose, Jetfrost, and Volt went to check it out more closely. When they removed the debris covering whatever it was, they were astonished to see it was no longer Dark Strike, but he had returned to being Obsidion.

As he became conscious, he noticed the three and asked, "Where am I? What's going on? Why are the three of you looking at me as though you've seen a ghost?"

Volt responded, "You mean, you can't remember?"

Obsidion nodded and responded, "No, honestly, I can't!" Looking around at all the destruction, he added, "Did I do all this?"

No one responded, letting him realize he was responsible for the massive damage. Guilt immediately sets in, causing him to hang his head in shame.

"What have I done to this world?"

Strike then said, "It wasn't you, Obsidion, it was Dark Strike who consumed you to do this! He no longer exists!" Strike held out his hand to Obsidion, saying, "You've returned to the family you belong to. Welcome home, brother!"

Curiously, Obsidion looked at Strike and asked, "Who are you?"

"Your new brother and friend," answered Strike. "I am Strike Dragon, the King of all Dragons."

Obsidion looked Strike in the eyes and took his reaching hand with glee.

Once Obsidion was on his feet, he said, "Thank you, brother, for giving me a second chance!"

Strike responded, "You're most welcome, Obsidion!"

With a grateful smile on his face, Obsidion said, "Actually, I no longer wish to be called Obsidion. I'd rather be called Leocore from now on if you don't mind."

"All right, consider it done," Strike answered.

Strike then lifted his arm and shook hands with Leocore.

Everyone cheered or roared with delight! Strike, hearing it all, let out a mighty roar of his own that echoed from building to building! Meanwhile, after hearing all that was going on, Slithor emerged and healed his own damaged arm. He is not happy with the outcome of things and clawed a nearby building out of frustration. Also, a damaged Dr. Syclonus appeared behind Slithor, to much surprise that he's still alive.

"Surprising that you survived, doctor," Slithor said in an amused voice.

The doctor responded, "I was lucky to survive in spite of a certain comrade that fired a missile launch! Damn that Sanus!"

The doctor said to Slithor, "Speaking of Sanus, how is he and the other generals? Did they even survive?"

Slithor, with a deep sigh, responded, "Two of our generals took serious damage, especially Gen. Oblivion. Is there a chance we can save them?"

The doctor responded, "There is a slim chance that they can be saved, but the problem is it will take a while to repair their bodies."

Slithor answered, "Then call all the psycho dragon droids in!"

The doctor then summoned them. They awakened from their slumber and entered the portal to head toward Earth. Four droids emerged and showed their respect by taking a knee. One of the droids, Gen. Dacktus, asked Slithor how can they be of service.

Slithor explained, "Two of our generals took serious damage as well as others on the team, and I want you to salvage them to the best of your ability."

Dr. Syclonus said, "What about Lord Dark Strike?"

Slithor, in a saddened voice, said, "I'm afraid he was defeated by the one who goes by the name of Strike Dragon."

They were all shocked to hear that their lord and master was defeated by one dragon.

One of the droids shouted, "How can one dragon defeat the King of the Shadows?"

Slithor explained, "Because he's no ordinary dragon, he's a SUPER Dragon!"

"Fascinating," said the doctor. "I never expected that Lord Dark Strike could be defeated at all, let alone by just one dragon!"

Slithor responded, "That's because Lord Dark Strike underestimated Strike's powers just as he did with his father!"

Gen. Dacktus chimed in, "So once we've salvaged as you ordered us to, what shall we do next?"

Slithor responded, "For now, we regroup and head back to base." He then announced to the group, "I assure all of you that once we return to base to repair and recover, we will have our revenge on the dragon who killed our Lord Dark Strike! For now, I will take command of the Shadow Dragons as your leader. Now, get a move on!"

They all collectively headed toward the portal with Slithor stopping just shy of the entrance and turning and staring in the direction of Strike in the distance, saying, "Don't think this is over, dragon! Not by a long shot!" He then continued entering the portal, and they vanished.

*****

ONE YEAR LATER... Humans and Dragon Knights alike work hard, hand in hand, together to repair the damage from the fierce battle. Everyone from the entire state came together to chip in on helping.

In a police station in San Francisco, an officer who is preparing to join helping looked at a photo of the family who raised him while sitting in the locker room.

A fellow officer entered and said, "Yo, Jet! It's time for us to go!"

The officer answered, "Okay, sure! I'll be there in a second."

Jet took one last look at the photo then gently placed it in his locker. He then grabbed his things and closed the locker door to reveal the initials "JS" on it for "Jet Speed."

Meanwhile, as San Diego is being repaired, they decided to remember the epic battle with a statue of Strike and Dark Strike engaging in combat. The statue brings mixed emotions from those who see it. Once the repairs of the city were complete, the Dragon Knights returned to Dragza. All except one. Strike. He felt it necessary to remain on Earth to continue protecting it. They all understand his position and accepted his decision to stay. He does, however, let the Dragon Knights know that, if needed, he will be right there to help them as their king.

Fast forward to the cemetery where Chuck is being laid to rest. All his friends and family are mourning his passing. Jack started it off by placing a flower on the casket. Everyone else followed, doing the same thing. Kari placed a special red rose of love on the casket. Kira placed a toy soldier on top of the casket given to him by Chuck when they were just kids. Chuck's headstone reads, "Charles 'Chuck' Johnson, Devoted Friend, Brother, and Son."

As time passed, everyone left the service except for Kari and Kira. They think back to when they all hung out as kids and what great memories they were. Kira thought about when he carried Chuck's body away from the scene when he was killed by Dark Strike. Kira noticed Kari crying as she stared at Chuck's grave and gently took one of his hands to comfort her.

They locked eyes and Kira said, "I know this is a very dark time for us, Kari, but you can count on me to honor Chuck's dying wish to look after you no matter what."

She responded in a sad voice, "I know you will, Kira. If only Chuck had told me sooner how he felt about me."

Kira responded, "Love can be so unpredictable. You just never know how it will or won't work out."

Kari, with a caring look on her face, said, "You mean, how you and I feel about each other?"

Kira explained, "I think Chuck knew about how you and I feel about each other, Kari, which is why he never let on how he really felt."

They both became silent for a minute before embracing with a passionate kiss. Meanwhile, Jack and Mia returned to see if Kari and Kira were all right and witnessed them kiss.

Jack said, "I knew it all along about you guys! You weren't fooling anyone!"

Mia chimed in, "You mean just like us, Jack?"

Jack, with an embarrassed look on his face, said softly, "Uh, I guess so."

Suddenly, a siren can be heard in the near distance.

Kari, knowing this is something Kira must check out, said, "I'll be all right, Kira. You go do what you do best!"

Kira kissed her on the forehead and said, "I'll be back before you know it!"

Kira turned and raced in the direction of the siren to see what it's all about.

While running and transforming at the same time, he said inside his own head as a narrative: "Well, now you know my story. As a teenage boy who has good friends and family while having a normal life, and the next thing you know, a crystal from another world chooses me to be a Dragon Superhero! I sometimes wonder why it chose me in the first place, but now I think I know why. The Spirit Core chose me because of my good heart I inherited from my parents, and my father felt me worthy of doing what's right. No matter what evil lurks out there, I will fight to defend the Multiverse. So this is Kira Scott, but you all know who I really am. I am Strike Dragon: The Last of the Light!"

Cut to a lab in San Diego. Roger, the archaeologist, is trying to contact Kira to let him know about another crystal he's discovered that seemed to be pure evil.

To be continued...

About the Author

Robert Edward Ashby was born in 1990 in Escondido, California. He was diagnosed with autism at an early age. Raised by his mom, Michelle, he has an older brother, Jesse, and a younger sister, Rachelle. Robert's family had many struggles and challenges throughout his life.

Robert has a big loving heart and a caring soul, along with an amazing imagination. He has always loved superheroes. Robert wants to live in a world where dragons rule because they protect the innocent and take on the evil that wants to destroy. When Robert was a teenager, he came up with his character, Strike Dragon. This is just the beginning of all the story that he has memorized in his head. There will be more to come.

Robert is a client of the San Diego Regional Center. Through their program with Options For All of San Diego, Robert has been learning to read. His day people, Taylor R. McElroy and Derek E. Shelton, were very beneficial in helping to type up the story that

Robert has in his head. Robert's mom tried helping to type it up but works a lot. Without the program's help, this would all be just a dream for Robert.

Robert is very excited that his dream is beginning to come true. He hopes to one day be able to provide for his family. He also dreams of one day being able to help other people and kids with autism and special needs too. Robert is a firm believer in always doing what is right and being kind!

CPSIA information can be obtained
at www.ICGtesting.com
Printed in the USA
BVHW050440130722
641931BV00002B/209